TOPZ SECRET STORIES

THE Cloudgate Mystery

Alexa Tewkesbury

CWR

Published 2013 by CWR, Waverley Abbey House, Waverley Lane, Farnham, Surrey
GU9 8EP, UK. Registered Charity No. 294387. Registered Limited Company No.
1990308.

See back of book for list of National Distributors.

All Scripture references are from the Good News Bible, copyright © American Bible
Society 1966, 1971, 1976, 1992, 1994.

Concept development, editing, design and production by CWR

Illustrations: Mike Henson at CWR

Printed in the UK by Page Brothers

ISBN: 978-1-85345-992-4

Hi there!
I'm Clyde – I'm in the Dixons Gang.

You might have heard of us. There's me and my mates, Rick and Kevin, and we all live on the Dixons Estate, in Holly Hill.

There's not that much to do in Holly Hill so we like to hang out together. The best places are the shopping centre and the park – there's lots of room there to play football or ride a bike.

Sometimes we run into the Topz Gang. 'Topzies' we call them just 'cos it bugs them. They're really annoying – they always seem to be talking about God and I don't get it. Us Dixons, we're cool. But Topz, they're just a waste of space.

It's weird, though. Something just happened that got me thinking about God. I mean, what if He really *does* exist? And if He does, could He ever really love someone like *me*?

That's what this story is all about ...

Hi! We're the Topz Gang –

Topz because we all live at the 'top' of something …
either in houses at the top of the hill, at the top of the
flats by the park, even sleeping in a top bunk counts!

We are all Christians, and we go to Holly Hill School.
We love Jesus, and try to work out our faith in God in
everything we do – at home, at school and with our
friends. That even means trying to show God's love to
the Dixons Gang who tend to be bullies, and can be a
real pain!

If you'd like to know more about us, visit our website
at www.cwr.org.uk/topz You can read all about us,
and how you can get to know and understand the Bible
more by reading our *Topz* notes, which are great fun,
and written every two months just for you!

One

The picture fell out of the book when Clyde opened it. He watched it glide to the floor, then bent down to pick it up. The piece of paper was folded into four. He smoothed it flat and gazed at the drawing. He'd forgotten this one.

It wasn't finished. Only half of it was coloured in. The rest was just pale, lightly pencilled outlines; a ghost of a picture.

Clyde's eyes ran over it. He'd obviously meant to finish the drawing. That's why he'd tucked it into a book. Perhaps he'd been interrupted or had run out of time or simply got bored. Still, what he'd drawn must have interested him enough to keep it to complete another day.

But this was a picture from some time ago. And the more Clyde stared at it, the more babyish it seemed. It didn't even really look like what it was meant to be.

Why had he kept it? It didn't deserve to be finished.

Impatiently, he tore it up, scrunched the pieces together into a tight ball and buried them carefully amongst the rubbish in the bin under his desk. He wanted to make sure no one found them. Clyde didn't like people looking at his pictures when he was *pleased* with them, let alone the ones he was ashamed of. As much as he could at home, he drew and painted in secret.

At school it was different. Whatever work you did in art, good or bad, everyone saw it. And usually, Clyde's was good. Even very good. He couldn't hide it. He stood out in his class.

'If you'd put even *half* the energy you put into your art into your other school work, you'd go a long way,' his teacher had said to him several times. 'Too busy being a Dixon, that's your trouble, Clyde.'

Being one of the Dixons Gang certainly took up Clyde's time. And it wasn't time well spent. He and the other two boys, Rick and Kevin, hung around together in school and out of it. They terrorised other kids in Holly Hill, and were forever landing themselves in trouble. Half the time, they weren't even that nice to each other.

Rick and Kevin teased Clyde unkindly when he tried hard at his art or made the effort to get any homework done on time. So sometimes, Clyde wouldn't do his homework at all, or he'd do it badly, just to try to show them that he didn't care about it.

The trouble was that he *did* care. He really did. He just didn't want anyone to know.

This week, Clyde's class had begun a project on legends. The homework was to choose a legend, write a version of the story and create a cover picture for it.

Rick and Kevin had groaned and rolled their eyes, but Clyde was excited. He didn't let anyone see it, and instead pulled a face like a true Dixon when the task was announced. But his heart began to beat that little bit faster and inside his head, he'd already begun to turn over possibilities.

Clyde couldn't care less about the story part. He didn't like reading or writing. It was hard work. His spelling was appalling and he knew it.

But the cover illustration! That was something he *could* do! Something he *wanted* to do.

Something he could lose himself in.

Clyde began to flick through the book where he'd found his drawing. It was a large, hard-backed and colourful collection of myths, legends and fairytales. His mum had come across it at a car boot sale and bought it for him. Clyde had always loved looking at pictures and the illustrations in this book were magical. Dragons and many-headed monsters and mysterious-looking castles and fearless knights on horseback. The images had always fascinated him. Now he wanted to invent a cover that would fascinate his teacher.

Suddenly, Clyde's phone bleeped. Instantly, he felt irritated. He didn't want the interruption. He reached across to his bed and checked the mobile. The text was from Rick.

What U doing?

Clyde raised his eyes. If Rick was asking what he was doing, he was probably at a loss for something to do himself.

He dropped the phone back on the bed without texting a reply. He'd spent that Saturday morning down at the park with Rick. All he wanted now was to look at the pictures in his book and plan what to draw for his story cover. If he didn't text back, hopefully Rick would assume he was busy and leave him alone.

He didn't.

Where R U?

Again Clyde ignored him.

Wherever U R get urself down the shopping centre. Something U gotta see.

Clyde was annoyed. Why couldn't Rick just leave him alone? Jabbing at the keys, he texted angrily: *What?*

Within seconds, Rick's answer bleeped back.

Just get down here!

Clyde looked at the time. Four o'clock. If he went now, maybe he could be back in an hour. Then he could get on with his homework. It wasn't as if he had any other plans.

'Going out, Mum!' he yelled as he pulled on his trainers by the front door.

He didn't wait for a reply. He never did. The slam of the door let his mum know that he'd gone.

The walkway that led into the shopping centre was smart and wide, and paved in pale grey slabs that gleamed when the sun shone and looked drab on dull days. Tuesday was market day, when a host of stalls were set up in rows across the slabs. Shoppers would thread their way through the network of paths that ran between them.

From time to time, too, when it wasn't clustered with market stalls, buskers appeared along the walkway; musicians who played and singers who sang. There had even been a living statue: a woman dressed as a Victorian lady, but all in pure white; pure white dress, face, white hair. She stood, frozen still, on a white-painted wooden crate until a passer-by dropped a coin into her basket, whereupon she would lower the white fan held to her face, smile at the giver and curtsy prettily. If it was a child who gave her money, she'd blow them a kiss.

'Clyde! Over here!'

Clyde had almost reached the walkway when Rick yelled at him. Still annoyed with the other Dixon for the interruption, Clyde stomped towards him.

Rick stood in the centre of the paved area, his arms spread wide and a huge grin all over his face.

He yelled again. 'What d'you think?'

Clyde had hardly snapped back, 'Why are you yelling? I can hear you!' – when he stopped short.

Spread across the paving slabs in front of Rick – drawn onto them – was a picture: a street scene. It showed several elegant-looking shop fronts and a café with a striped canopy and a scattering of little tables and chairs spilling out onto the pavement. There were two small trees in pots either side of the café entrance door, and a lady in a long yellow dress sat at one of the tables, a little black dog tied to the leg of her chair.

Clyde's eyes flicked backwards and forwards as he tried to take it all in. He'd seen pavement art on the internet but never in real life. It was an unusual thing to come across in Holly Hill. And this scene was perfect! So perfect he felt he could almost step into it, sit down next to the lady in yellow and stroke the little dog.

'Pretty cool, eh?' said Rick. 'Told you you had to get down here.'

Clyde's eyes were still glued to the picture. The lines and colours were soft; powdery. They looked like chalk.

Other people gazed down at the scene, too. Everyone admired it. It was so beautiful and unexpected, they seemed almost startled by it.

Clyde moved around the picture until he stood next to Rick.

'Who did this?' he asked.

Rick shrugged. 'Dunno. I only came out to get some milk for Mum and I found it. Seems a bit of a waste, though,' he added. 'As soon as it rains, it'll get washed away.'

'It's incredible!' Clyde whispered. He was still stunned.

Suddenly he looked up and glanced around at all the faces wondering at the picture, too. Could one of these people be the artist? Clyde's eyes searched the audience.

No, these were shoppers with carrier bags, or people simply passing through. Their breath had been taken away by the picture, just as his had. None of them had created it.

'I wish I had a decent phone,' Clyde muttered. 'Then I could take a photo.'

'Sorry,' replied Rick. 'Can't help. My phone's even more rubbish than yours.'

Clyde had to content himself with holding the image in his head until he got back to the Dixons Estate.

As soon as he was home, he raced up to his room, sat at his desk and tried to sketch out a version of the scene. He pencilled in the shop fronts, the café, the chairs and tables, the lady in yellow and the dog. He held up the piece of paper in front of him to have a proper look at what he'd done.

He didn't like it. To his eyes, the sketch was nothing like the pavement picture. It was one of those drawings of his he'd normally have thrown away.

But this time he didn't.

What he'd drawn wasn't important. What mattered was the image it reminded him of, and the way that image had made him feel.

'Where did you go shooting off to all of a sudden?' Clyde's mum, Cathy, asked when he sat down to supper later.

'Only the shopping centre,' he said. 'Rick texted. There was this picture someone had done on the ground.'

'Huh!' scoffed his dad. 'Graffiti! It's everywhere. People making a mess and forcing others to have to look at it!'

'No.' Clyde shook his head. 'It wasn't graffiti, it was pavement art. There's a difference. Anyway, some graffiti artists are really clever, too.'

'It's a mess that needs scrubbing off,' his dad, Rob, insisted as if Clyde hadn't spoken.

Everyone ate in silence for a few moments.

Finally Cathy asked, 'So what was this picture you saw?'

'It was incredible!' Clyde said. 'It was a street. And there was a lady in a yellow dress and she had a dog.'

'Are we talking about the picture or someone you saw when you were out?' his dad said. He took a last mouthful of mashed potato.

Clyde sighed. He wished he hadn't mentioned it. No one would take him seriously. No one would care about it the way he did.

'The picture, Rob!' Cathy said firmly. 'Go on, then, Clyde, tell us some more.'

Clyde finished eating and put his knife and fork down on the empty plate.

'It doesn't matter,' he said. 'It was a picture and I liked it, and I've got no idea who did it.'

'I have.' Clyde's half-sister, Ashley, was sitting opposite him at the table.

'Did you see it?' he asked. 'Did you see someone drawing it?'

'I didn't have to,' Ashley said. 'There's a girl at school. She did it. She's called Lizzi Brewer. She's in the year above me.'

'But it was such an amazing picture.' Clyde shook his head. 'The person who drew it *can't* still be at school.'

'Well, she is,' Ashley answered offhandedly. 'Apparently she's got a place at some summer school of art in Paris in August. She's going to be doing pavement art and portraits and stuff to raise some money to help pay for it.'

'I can't believe it,' Clyde murmured. 'I can't believe you know her!'

'We both do art, so of course I know her,' grunted Ashley. 'Sometimes I wish I didn't.'

'Why?' asked Clyde.

'I think everyone at Bruford gets sick of the sound of her name. Her stuff's up everywhere. Sketches and paintings. I think it's really unfair. There are loads of us doing art, but mention Lizzi Brewer and all the teachers go weak at the knees.' Ashley pursed her lips. 'I don't understand it. It's not even as if she's that good.'

Clyde frowned. 'Not that good? That picture down at the shopping centre was brilliant!'

'Sounds like a bit of a teacher's pet to me,' said Rob. 'She can't be that great if Ashley doesn't rate her. After all, our Ashley here's a *proper* artist. Aren't you, Ashley?'

Two

When Ashley was little, she was always painting and drawing and colouring. She'd lost interest after Rob and her own mum had separated, but eventually she'd picked it up again, and now art was her favourite subject at Bruford Secondary School.

Her teacher, Mr Keller, always encouraged her. He encouraged everyone – but he'd get especially excited about pupils with that 'extra special razzmatazz' as he called it.

The 'extra special razzmatazz', Clyde always assumed when it was mentioned, was the difference between simply *doing* art and actually *shining* at it.

Ashley seemed to be one of those that shone, and her dad was hugely proud of the fact.

It was pure coincidence that art had turned out to be the one thing Clyde enjoyed at Southlands Primary School, too; the one thing he was ever praised for by his teacher.

But art was Ashley's 'thing' and it always seemed to Clyde that their dad thought more of what Ashley achieved than anything *he* ever did, especially since she'd come to live with them. So why would he take Clyde's scribbles seriously? He'd probably think they were nothing beside his daughter's.

That's what Clyde thought, too, a lot of the time. That's why he shut himself away in his room to draw. If no one in his family could see, then no one could compare.

When Southlands had held an exhibition recently of all the best artwork in the school for that year, three of Clyde's pictures had been chosen. Children were given invitations to give to their parents or carers. They were asked to come into school one evening to see the display.

But Clyde's parents never saw his invitation. He didn't even take it home. Clyde didn't want them to see his artwork. Certainly not his dad, who was bound to criticise. That's if he was interested enough to come at all. The next day, Clyde simply told his teacher that they wouldn't be there. They were both busy.

A few weeks before, however, someone in his family did see one of his pictures.

Clyde had been drawing in his bedroom. He was so absorbed in his sketch that he didn't hear Ashley creep up behind him. She stood for a few moments, watching over his shoulder.

As soon as he realised she was there, he hastily flipped the paper over.

It was too late, of course.

'No, don't hide it,' Ashley had said. 'I was looking.'

'You shouldn't come in my room without knocking,' Clyde muttered. 'I don't do that to you.'

'What are you drawing?' Ashley asked. 'Just tell me what the picture's meant to be and then I'll leave you alone.'

'It doesn't matter,' Clyde replied, wishing he'd heard her come in; that there'd been time to hide his drawing before her steely eyes had caught sight of it.

'No, go on, tell me,' said Ashley. 'I really want to know.'

Clyde shook his head. 'It's nothing,' he mumbled.

Ashley stared at him silently for a moment. Then, 'You're right,' she said. 'It *is* nothing. Don't try to be like me, Clyde. You never will be, you know. You just haven't got what it takes.'

That was one of Clyde's drawings that had ended up in the bin; torn to shreds and angrily crushed in his hands as though he was trying to squeeze the life out of it.

In fact the last person in the world Clyde wanted to be like was Ashley. The two of them put up with each other because they had to. They shared a dad and more recently they'd had to learn to share a house. But it wasn't easy. It wasn't comfortable. Ashley was a few years older than Clyde and he longed for the day when she was a few years older still. Old enough to leave home.

No, being like Ashley was the last thing Clyde wanted.

But he did want to draw and paint. More and more, when he grew up, he felt he wanted to be an artist.

First thing the next morning, Clyde looked out of the window.

'No!' he murmured.

It had rained in the night. Not much, but everywhere looked damp. Rain would have fallen on the pavement picture and spoilt it.

Clyde threw on his clothes and slipped out through the front door. It was Sunday morning and early. No one else in the house was awake. Even outside everything was so still Clyde thought perhaps no one else in the whole street was awake.

Nearer the shopping centre, too, there were very few people about. But then on Sundays nothing opened until ten o'clock, so why would there be?

The picture hadn't been washed away. It was smudged and the colours had blurred into each other, but it was still a perfect street scene. The rain had simply given it a kind of hazy look.

'I think I like it better now it's been rained on.'

Clyde turned his head. The girl who'd spoken stood a little way away from him. She had long red hair twisted into a plait that hung to one side of her head and fell over her shoulder. She obviously didn't feel the cold. Although it was May, the last few days had been cool for the time of year. It was cool now, but she stood there in just shorts, t-shirt and flip-flops.

Clyde felt awkward. He'd wanted to be able to look at the image on his own; to study it properly before it *did* get washed away. He didn't feel like talking.

'I liked it before it got rained on,' he muttered finally, and thrust his hands into the pockets of his hoodie.

There. He'd answered. Now maybe the girl would go away.

She didn't.

'So, what do you think of it?' she asked.

Clyde shrugged. 'I told you. I like it.'

'Yeah, but what do you *think* of it?' the girl persisted. 'Personally, I'm not sure about the yellow dress. And I think maybe one tree would be better by the café door. And let's face it, the dog's just ridiculous.'

Clyde glanced at her. Who did she think she was, pulling the picture apart like that? 'Well, I *like* the dog,' he said. 'And the dress. And there's nothing wrong with having two trees.'

'You think,' said the girl. She gazed at the picture with her head on one side – the same side as the plait, so that it looked a little as if the weight of her hair was pulling her head over. 'Do you know a lot about art?'

'No,' Clyde said. 'I just know what I like.'

'So what do you like about this? Go on, tell me. I'm interested.'

Clyde gave her a sideways look. 'Why do you care what *I* think?'

The girl straightened her head and looked back at him. 'I just think pictures should be talked about. Don't you?'

To Clyde, that made sense. Pictures *were* something to be talked about. But apart from his teacher at Southlands, he'd never really had anyone to talk about them with.

He nodded. 'OK,' he said. 'I like the colours. I don't know why you don't like the yellow dress, because I think it's just right. It's the only thing that's yellow in the whole picture. It makes the lady stand out. Really stand out. Like she's special or something. And I like the way she's sitting there with her dog because that makes her real. A *real* person with *real* life stuff going on like having a dog. And I like the way the shops don't look like any shops I've ever seen round here.'

Clyde hesitated a moment, thinking. Then, 'And you're wrong about the trees,' he added. 'Two trees, one either side of the café door – that's what the doorway needs. If there was only one it would look like something was missing. At least it would to me.' He paused again. 'But I think what I *really* like – more than all the rest of it – is that … I wanna walk along that street … I wanna be in that picture because it's perfect …'

He trailed off. Suddenly he felt embarrassed.

'Anyway, that's it,' he finished bluntly. 'That's what I think. That's what I like. Good enough for you?'

'Interesting,' the girl said. 'I suppose maybe what's perfect for one person is never going to be perfect for someone else.'

'Well, it should be,' Clyde muttered.

A few other people had stopped to look at the picture. He hoped none of them had heard what he'd said about it.

'Do you like to draw?' the girl asked.

'Why do you want to know?' Clyde retorted.

'Do you, though?'

'I dunno. Sometimes. Doesn't everyone like to draw sometimes?'

'And do you like *what* you draw?' the girl continued.

Clyde was getting fed up. This was too many questions. 'Not really. In fact, most of the time, not at all. Anyway, what's it got to do with you?' he snapped.

'Because some people might think *your* drawings are perfect,' the girl smiled. 'But if you drew them, they're probably never going to be perfect for you.'

Clyde stared at her for a moment; dug his hands deeper into his pockets. A dampness drifted across his face. It had started to rain again. A fine drizzle floated lightly on the air.

'I've gotta go,' he said.

'Yeah, well, it was good to talk to you.' The girl smiled. She glanced up towards the sky. 'Shame about the weather. Looks like it won't be long before your idea of a perfect picture has been drizzled away.'

Three

The wet weather didn't last. It got warmer, too. The following Saturday was the warmest day of spring so far, and the park teemed with people. Everywhere there were children, running, laughing; on the play equipment, in the sand pit, in the skateboard park. There wasn't a spare seat to be had on the benches. Groups sprawled on the newly-cut grass, chatting or reading or sleeping, or simply lapping up the sunshine.

Two boys sat cross-legged side by side on the ground at the far end of the park near the tennis courts. They were bent over a large sketchpad, lost in concentration.

'What about tunnels?' said the boy with glasses. Behind the lenses, his eyes sparkled with excitement. 'Tunnels would be awesome!'

'Yup, tunnels would be cool,' agreed the other. 'Just not sure if we can be that ... well ... complicated.'

'What's complicated about tunnels?' asked the first boy. 'You get them on railway lines all the time.'

His friend glanced at him. 'That's probably because they sort of *have* to be there,' he replied. 'I mean, you need them on railway lines, don't you? Because of roads running over the top of them and stuff. But this is a cycle track we're talking about, Paul. I think our ideas are supposed to be ... sensible.'

Paul adjusted his glasses. 'Or boring,' he sighed.

There had been a big article in the local paper that week about the decision to build a cycle track in the park at Holly Hill. Anyone under eighteen had been invited to send in their suggestions for what they'd like to see included in the design.

Paul and his friend, Dave, had been poring over the sketchpad for the last hour. So far they'd come up with a kind of bike obstacle course with a lot of steep humps, but not much else.

Suddenly Paul brightened again. 'What about a row of posts?' he said. 'You know, spaced out so you can weave in and out of them?'

Dave thought about it. 'Great idea,' he nodded. 'How many d'you think?'

Paul didn't answer the question. His brain had already leapt on to something else.

'A water splash!' he shrieked. 'We've just gotta have a water splash!'

This time Dave looked slightly doubtful again. 'I suppose,' he nodded, 'but is everyone really going to want to cycle through something that gets them all wet?'

'Well, yeah, why wouldn't they?' Paul grinned. 'We could put it at the bottom of one of the ramps. When we hit it, it'll make a tidal wave!'

Paul was just about to point to a spot on their sketch design where the water splash could go, when the pad Dave was drawing on was suddenly launched into the air.

'Woo hoo!' yelled the boy, whose kick had sent it flying. 'Who cares that I forgot to bring my football? I can use this!'

The boy ran over to where the pad had landed. Paul and Dave hardly had time to scramble to their feet before another kick had shot it even further away across the grass. The boy watched them.

'Oh no!' he said, stretching his eyes wide, as if he was scared. 'Are the Topzy boys coming after me?'

Another boy ran up. It was Rick from the Dixons Gang. 'Over here, Kev!' he shouted.

Kevin, who'd thrown the first kick, gave the pad another sharp jab with the toe of his trainer. He sent it in Rick's direction. It didn't fly so far this time, but the top sheet of paper ripped almost right the way across. Paul and Dave's design for the bike track was torn in two and hung on by a corner.

The two Dixons bent double with laughter. Paul and Dave were members of another Holly Hill gang called Topz. Dixons hated them. If they could find a way to mess up their days, then that's what they'd do.

Clyde, the third Dixon, was there, too, but he hung back.

Dave made a run for the pad but Rick was closer and got there first.

'Aww!' Rick said. He picked it up and glanced at the sketch. 'Have you been drawing pictures? Sweet!'

Before Dave could stop him, Rick had taken hold of one corner of the torn page and let the rest of the sketchpad drop. The paper ripped away from its other half completely. Rick stood holding it with a stupid grin on his face.

'Whoops!' he smirked. 'Oh well, never mind, eh? Your drawing looks rubbish!'

Kevin howled with laughter.

Dave took a step closer and snatched up the pad.

Rick watched him. 'Here,' he said. 'Catch!'

In a second, he'd scrunched what was left of the cycle track sketch into a ball and thrown it. Dave didn't catch it. Paul did.

'Ooh!' Kevin hooted scornfully. 'Looks like your speccies are working for you today, then, Paul!'

'Let's get out of here,' mumbled Dave. Paul nodded. The pair of them started to traipse away.

'Don't go!' wailed Rick. 'Was it something we said?'

Paul and Dave didn't look back; didn't glance at Clyde as they passed him by.

'D'you want to come to my house?' Paul asked Dave when they were out of earshot. 'We can draw the track out again. It won't take long. We know what we want.'

Dave shook his head. 'Nah,' he said. 'Not really in the mood any more. Maybe later.'

'They're just stupid, you know, Dixons,' said Paul. 'We can't let them get to us.'

'I know,' answered Dave. He forced a smile. 'Sometimes they do, though. Don't they?'

Dave didn't feel like going home. Instead he left Paul and wandered off in the direction of the shopping centre. If only Holly Hill was bigger, he thought. If only there were two parks, then Dixons could use one and Topz could use the other. If only the Dixons Estate was miles away from here instead of just up the road. Then they might *never* have to bump into each other. Topz might *never* have to see Dixons' stupid faces ever again!

If only Dixons didn't exist …

Dave rounded the corner and spotted a group of people gathered on the paved walkway that led down to the shops. That's when he remembered the picture that had appeared there last weekend. His friends from Topz, Sarah and Josie, had been so full of it that the whole gang had turned out to have a look.

'We saw the artist!' Sarah had said. 'I mean, she was actually there while *we* were. Actually doing the picture. We saw her colour the yellow dress in! She's *so* clever. And she's not even that old!'

Seeing the small crowd in front of him, Dave

wondered if the pavement artist was back. He cut across the walkway to join the onlookers.

Kneeling on a cushion on the ground was a teenage girl. She had a tray of different coloured pastels beside her and was shading in the outlines of an armchair. In the armchair sat a lady with blue-black hair piled on top of her head. One ringlet hung down. She gazed lovingly at a cat, the same colour as her hair, sprawled in her lap. With one hand she stroked its head. Next to the lady, the artist had drawn a large, rectangular mirror. It reflected almost the whole of her picture. There were just parts of the shading that weren't quite finished.

Dave gazed at the entire scene, astonished. Art was something he did at school because he had to. He didn't particularly enjoy it or *not* enjoy it. It was just something that *was*. Pictures and paintings had never really struck him in any particular way.

But *this* picture – spread out before him on the walkway, created before his very eyes – *this* picture was magical.

The girl looked up briefly at her audience. She smiled.

'Won't be long now,' she said. 'So who reckons it's going to rain as soon as I'm finished?'

A ripple of laughter ran through the onlookers.

'No, not today, love,' answered a cheerful-looking woman. 'It'll be all right. That lady in her armchair'll still be good as new tomorrow.'

'Hope so,' grinned the girl. 'Because that cat in her lap will not be happy if he gets wet!'

Dave chuckled along with the rest of the crowd.

A few people started to wander away towards the shops, but before they did, they chinked several coins into the basket the girl had placed at one corner of the picture.

'Thank you!' she called after them. Then she bent her head and continued to work.

Dave wanted to say something to her. Just to let her know what he thought of her pictures.

'Erm ...' he began awkwardly. 'Your drawings are fantastic. I loved the one last week, too. I mean, I didn't see you do it, but I guess it was you. You must have been gutted when it rained.'

The girl squinted up at him, the sun full in her eyes.

'No, not really,' she said. 'If I wanted it to last forever, I wouldn't have drawn it on a pavement.'

Dave shifted uncomfortably. He wasn't sure if she was teasing him.

'No, seriously,' she smiled. 'I could work out here on paper. You know, just tape it down and then have a picture to sell when I've finished. But the thing is, I'm new to this so I just thought I'd do a bit of experimenting first. Don't want to be trying to sell duds! Everybody's really getting into it already, though. I'm amazed.'

She stood up and wiped the back of her hand across her forehead.

'Wow, isn't it hot! Who'd have thought it after *last* weekend? Just a minute.' The girl stepped over to a large holdall, unzipped it and pulled out a baseball cap. She returned to Dave as she yanked it down onto her head. 'I should have put this on hours ago. Mum's always saying, "Don't forget to wear your hat if you're in the sun for long!" But I do forget. Get carried away with my pastels and end up with a stinking headache!'

Suddenly, she seemed to notice the sketchpad in Dave's hand.

'Oh, hello?' she said. 'Are you an artist, too?'

Dave shook his head quickly. 'No! No, not at all … I was just … with a friend. We were messing about, that's all. It's not even my pad, it's my dad's.'

'So your dad's the artist?'

'No, he's … no.'

The girl waited expectantly, but Dave had run out of things to say.

'OK, then.' She gave him a final smile. 'Well, I'd better get on or this lady and her cat are never going to have a complete armchair to sit in.'

She dropped down onto the cushion again to carry on.

Dave watched for a few moments more, then turned away to head into the shopping centre.

Instantly, he stopped short.

A little way in front of him, standing apart from the group of onlookers but with a clear view of the girl working on the picture, stood Clyde. He stared at her with a strange expression on his face; confusion mixed with annoyance. He didn't appear to notice Dave, much to the Topz boy's relief, who wasn't in the mood for another run-in with Dixons.

As Dave sloped away, he grasped the sketchpad a little more tightly.

'Why didn't you tell me?' he heard Clyde ask.

'Tell you what?' returned the girl.

Dave took one brief glance back over his shoulder. He didn't much care what the street artist hadn't told Clyde. Right then, all he wanted was to be nowhere near a Dixon.

28

Four

'You know what I'm talking about,' said Clyde, standing right up close to the girl, eyeing her accusingly. 'Why didn't you tell me it was you who did that picture last week?'

A number of people still watched as the girl added a last few strokes of green to the armchair she was shading. All that was left now was to finish the reflected version of the chair in the mirror.

She peered up at Clyde from under the peak of her baseball cap. 'Oh, it's you,' she smiled, suddenly recognising him. 'You're the boy who wanted to step into my street scene.'

Clyde asked again. 'Why didn't you tell me it was *your* picture?'

The girl stood up, tucking a stray strand of red hair behind her ear. 'I think that would have been a bit like bragging, wouldn't it?'

Clyde frowned. 'But I told you what I thought. *Everything* I thought. I wouldn't have done that if I'd known.'

'Exactly,' the girl replied. 'And it's the *everything* that people think that's so interesting.'

'I never said anything bad, though. I only said good stuff.'

'I know. But good *or* bad, people never seem to talk quite so honestly about a picture when they know it's yours.'

'You should have told me,' Clyde muttered.

'I just wanted your honest opinion.'

'You still should have told me.'

The girl smiled to herself, moved the cushion she'd been kneeling on over to the mirror in her scene and began to shade the reflected armchair.

Clyde kicked at the ground with the toe of one trainer. 'I must have sounded like a right idiot,' he said sulkily.

'No!' The girl glanced up at him again. 'Why would you think that?'

Clyde didn't answer. Then, 'You're Lizzi Brewer, aren't you?' he said.

'That's me,' replied the girl. 'How did you know? Have you been asking around?'

'Ashley Bicton. She's my – well – my half-sister.' Clyde mumbled the words. He never liked telling people about Ashley. He wished she was nothing to do with him. 'Ashley told me.'

The girl continued to work on the reflection of the chair. A few more shoppers wandered over to watch. When anyone walked away, more often than not, they dropped a coin or two into the collecting basket as they left.

'I never knew Ashley had a half-brother,' Lizzi said.

'Well, she does and it's me,' Clyde grunted.

'Not that we talk to each other much,' Lizzi added. 'I don't think your half-sister's very keen on me.'

Lizzi was right. Clyde knew it. He remembered Ashley's scornful expression when she'd mentioned how Lizzi was going to raise some money to help pay for her trip to Paris and the summer school; what she'd said about being sick of the sound of Lizzi's name.

'How d'you know that?' Clyde asked.

'Oh, you must know your own half-sister,' Lizzi replied, still not taking her eyes off her work. 'She's not one for keeping her feelings to herself.'

Clyde grinned. 'Yeah,' he agreed.

Almost instantly he started to like the girl with the long red plait and the baseball cap.

Lizzi stood up and took a couple of steps back. 'Da-dah! Finished!' she announced.

There was a burst of applause from the straggle of onlookers. She smiled round at them, said thank you and dropped the pastel she'd been using into the tray with the other colours.

Lizzi looked back at Clyde. 'I don't even know your name,' she said.

'Clyde.'

'Clyde?' she repeated. 'Unusual.'

Clyde shrugged.

'The Clyde's a river in Scotland, isn't it?' Lizzi said.

'Yup,' Clyde replied. 'I'm named after it.'

'Named after a river, that's so cool,' said Lizzi. She pushed back her cap, folded her arms and gazed down at the picture she'd just created. 'So, Clyde-named-after-a-river, what do you think of this one?'

Clyde threw her a sideways look. 'But I know it's yours so how can I be "honest"?'

Lizzi laughed. 'Huh! Cheeky one, aren't you? Go on,' she said. 'Just say the first thing that comes into your head.'

Clyde stared at the scene. The lady with blue-black hair sitting serenely in the chair; the blue-black cat in her lap, comfortable, relaxed; the mirror calmly repeating the image almost exactly.

'I like it,' he said quietly.

'Because …?' Lizzi waited.

Suddenly, Clyde realised she was right. Now that he knew Lizzi was the artist, it *was* harder to say exactly what he thought. He felt awkward somehow; self-conscious.

'Because ...' He shook his head. 'Because I just like it.'

Lizzi smiled. 'Well, I guess that's a reason.'

She bent down to pick up the tray of pastels and the cushion. She unzipped the holdall and began to pack away.

'I hope that means you're not cross with me any more,' she said.

'What do you mean?' Clyde frowned. 'I wasn't cross with you.'

Lizzi laughed. 'Oh, I think you were. When you first got here. I think you thought I'd played a trick on you by not telling you who I was last week.'

'I didn't!' said Clyde. 'Well, maybe I was a bit cross, but it doesn't matter.'

'Good,' she grinned. She grabbed the little basket that held the coins people had been leaving. 'Now,' she said, 'help me count these up, would you? I may be OK at art but my maths is terrible.'

Dave slumped down onto his bed. He felt fed up. Miserable. Another perfectly good day wrecked by the Dixons Gang. It was weird how sometimes he could shrug them off and not care at all, whatever they said; whatever they did. But there were other times when all he wanted was to hide away from them; lock the door, close the curtains, curl up into a ball and literally hide.

He glanced at the sketchpad he'd dropped on the bed beside him. A remnant of his and Paul's sketch design for the new cycle track still clung to it. He grabbed at it, ripped it off and tore it up.

What is the point of the Dixons Gang, God?

Dave began to pray as he screwed up the bit of paper, reached over to his wastepaper bin and threw it in.

*What's the point? Why are they here? We weren't doing anything, Paul and me. We weren't in anyone's way. We were just **there**, God, in the park – but they couldn't leave us alone, could they?*

*I don't know why any of us Topz keep going down there. Dixons act like they own the place. Always trying to get rid of us. I don't even know why I'm excited about the cycle track. It's stupid to get excited, isn't it? Even if any of our ideas for it get built, we'll never be able to use it. We'll never get to try it out. Because Dixons will **always** be there – kicking balls at us, standing in the way, staring, shouting. They'll make it **their** cycle track. It won't just be us either. They'll spoil it for everybody.*

I wish You could just tell me, God – WHAT ARE DIXONS FOR? They don't do anything useful. They never do anything 'nice'. They're just mean the whole time.

I know You've got a plan for each of us. You have, haven't You? That's what it says in the Bible. There's a plan. You've given us all different gifts and if we try to live the way You want, You'll show us what they are and how we can use them for You.

What's Your plan for Dixons, God? Is there one? Have they got any 'gifts'? As far as I can see, all they're good at is being nasty and screwing up people's days and putting them in bad moods! Maybe they'll never know what You want for them because they take no notice of You. Maybe that's it – and they'll just never find out.

So like I say, God – **what is the point of the Dixons Gang?**

Five

First thing on Sunday morning, Clyde was back at the shopping centre. He bought himself a doughnut at the baker's and hung around near the lady in the green armchair. It had been a dry night so the picture still lay across the walkway, untouched.

'You're here bright and early,' said a voice. Lizzi strolled towards him, her holdall in one hand, the other tucked into the pocket of her shorts. Her hair, in its usual long, thick plait, was tied at the end with a red-and-white striped ribbon.

'You said I could watch you draw today,' answered Clyde. 'Didn't want to miss anything.'

Lizzi nodded towards the doughnut in his hand. 'I see you don't believe in a healthy breakfast?'

Clyde shrugged. 'I just like doughnuts. Why? What did *you* have for breakfast?'

'A couple of bananas with yoghurt and honey,' Lizzi replied.

'Sounds a bit *too* healthy, if you ask me,' Clyde grunted.

Lizzi set down the holdall. She put her hands on her hips and gazed round at the paved area. She pointed.

'I think I might try and do something over there,' she said. 'What do you reckon, Clyde? Don't want to be too close to yesterday's.'

Clyde nodded. He liked the way Lizzi asked him what he thought. It didn't often happen. He'd never really felt his opinions were important. Lizzi treated him as if they were.

'Actually, d'you know what?' Lizzi said. 'It's really quiet out here yet. I think I might grab a coffee before I get started. D'you want to come?'

Again, Clyde nodded. 'Yeah, I'll come,' he said.
'But I don't like coffee.'

On the bench outside the baker's, Lizzi sipped her
large, frothy, takeaway latte and Clyde munched on
another doughnut.

'So, do you do much art at school?' Lizzi asked.

'Not as much as I'd like,' Clyde said. 'We do a bit.'

'Are you any good?'

'No, not really,' Clyde muttered.

'You really enjoy it, though, don't you?' Lizzi said. 'I bet you're better than you think you are.'

'I dunno,' he mumbled through a mouthful of doughnut. 'I never have any ideas. I just do what I'm told. You have loads of ideas.'

'Not always,' said Lizzi. 'Sometimes I sit down to draw and my mind's blank. Can't think of anything. I close my eyes and there's nothing there.'

'What are you drawing today?' Clyde asked.

Lizzi giggled. 'It's one of those blank mind days. Haven't a clue! Why do you think I wanted to grab a coffee?'

'Is it helping?'

'Not yet.'

There were a few more people around now. Shop owners were unlocking doors and shutters. The shopping centre was waking up.

'Do you people-watch, Clyde?' Lizzi asked suddenly.

Clyde looked puzzled. 'What d'you mean?'

'Do you watch people?' Lizzi said. 'Watch how they walk … Are they in a hurry or have they got all the time in the world? If they're in a hurry – why? Where have they been? Where are they going? If they look stressed – why? If they look happy – why? What's just happened? Are they on their own? Have they got family? People-watching,' she added. 'I do it all the time.'

Clyde stared at her. 'Isn't that the same as being nosey?'

'No, river boy, it's not!' laughed Lizzi. 'You can get so many ideas from watching people. Stories. The world's full of stories; did you know that?'

She took a long sip of coffee.

'Is that where the lady in the yellow dress came from?' Clyde asked. 'And the other one in the armchair? Did you see them somewhere?'

'Kind of.' Lizzi nodded. 'I saw a lady sitting outside a café a few weeks ago. But she didn't have a dog, and she wasn't wearing yellow, she was wearing brown. And she wasn't happy. She was on her mobile and she was crying. So I thought if I put her in a picture, I could *make* her happy.'

'What about the armchair lady?'

'Saw her in the window of a furniture shop. She must have been trying out the armchair or something. But there was a mirror on the wall beside her – a huge mirror with a gold frame. And there she was, reflected in the mirror, too, but she didn't know because she was looking the other way. So,' Lizzi said, 'I gave her a bit of a makeover, a cat, a far comfier chair than the one in the shop, and a room of her own to sit in. And then I did it all over again with the reflection.'

'Clever,' Clyde said. 'Really clever.'

'It's not!' Lizzi replied. 'Like I say, it's just stories; people-watching. I think, who are you and what can I make you into?'

'Still clever, though. I'm not as clever as that.'

Lizzi looked at him thoughtfully. 'Course you are,' she said. 'So, come on, then. What's *your* story, Clyde?'

'Why? Are you gonna draw me?'

'I will if you want me to.'

'Uh – no!' said Clyde.

What would Rick and Kevin say, he wondered, if the next time they went to the shopping centre, they found his face splashed all over the walkway? What would *Ashley* say?

'Ashley likes art, too, doesn't she?' Lizzi said. 'She's good, you know. Her style's a lot different to mine, but she's really good.'

Clyde thought about saying, 'That's not what Ashley says about you', but he didn't. It might hurt Lizzi's feelings, and that's not what he wanted.

'If she's your half-sister, who do you both share?' Lizzi continued. 'A mum or a dad?'

Why did Lizzi have to start talking about Ashley? Clyde had been enjoying himself until then.

'A dad,' he grunted.

'Is he artistic?'

'No. Why?'

'I always wonder,' Lizzi said thoughtfully, 'if you can draw or paint or write ... or act or sing – anything creative like that – where does it come from? Is it from one of your parents, or both of them? Or your grandparents, or even further back than that?' She paused. 'Or is it just there – in you?'

'Well, where d'*you* get it from?' Clyde asked. 'Is one of *your* parents an artist?'

Lizzi shook her head and lifted her shoulders. 'Don't ask me,' she said. 'I haven't the faintest idea.'

'What's up, Dave?' asked Greg.

Sunday Club was over. Dave and Josie helped the leader to stack chairs.

'He won't tell you,' said Josie. 'We've all been asking.'

Dave said nothing.

'Well, something's up,' said Greg. 'You look …
disgruntled.'

Dave looked at him. 'Dis-what?' he replied.

'Gruntled,' said Greg. 'Disgruntled.'

'I like that word,' said Josie.

'So you should,' answered Greg. 'It's a great word is
"disgruntled". I think we should all use it more often.'

'And it means … ?' asked Dave.

'It means annoyed. Fed up.'

'Just like your face, Dave,' added Josie.

'I'm all right,' muttered Dave. 'I can't help my face,
can I?'

The last chair was stacked.

'Thanks for your help, Josie,' said Greg. 'Off you
go now.'

Dave went to follow her but Greg called him back.
'I heard what happened with Dixons yesterday.
Paul told me.'

'Why?' frowned Dave. 'There was nothing to tell.
Anyway, I've forgotten about it.'

'Is that why you look disgruntled? Because you've
forgotten about it?'

Dave sighed. No matter how much you didn't feel like
talking about something, Greg had this way of getting
you to open up.

'Come on, Dave, what is it? It's not like you to let
Dixons get on top of you.'

Finally, Dave blurted it out. 'It's just so unfair! They
never leave us alone! It's not *their* park, it's *our* park,
too. It's *everyone's* park! But the minute you're in there
when they are, they're trying to get rid of you! I don't
get why God even made them. I keep asking Him what
they're here for.'

'Like wasps,' Greg smiled. 'I hate killing them but when I'm trying to get one out of the window and it just won't go, I do catch myself thinking, "What are you for?"'

'And what's the answer?' Dave said.

'In the case of wasps, I'm not sure there is one,' Greg shrugged. 'In the case of Dixons – or any of us, really – only God knows. You see, you and me, we can ask God what He wants us to do; how we can follow His plan for our lives, whatever that may be. Even if it's not clear to us, at least if we're living the way He asks us to in the Bible – being the kind of people He wants us to be – then we can be sure that He's guiding us and leading us.'

Greg paused and shook his head. 'But it's not for us to know God's plans for those Dixons boys. All we can do is keep praying for them; keep asking God to help them to find Him. Because it's only once they start talking to Him, once they start getting to know Him – once they're prepared to give their lives to Him – that He'll be able to begin properly leading them in the direction He wants them to go.'

Dave didn't answer.

'Look in your Bible when you get home,' Greg said. 'Jeremiah chapter 29 and verse 11. God says: *"I alone know the plans I have for you, plans to bring you prosperity and not disaster, plans to bring about the future you hope for."* That's an incredible verse! One of my favourites! Read it for yourself. Keep on reading it. None of us knows what God's plans are, Dave. But what we do know – you and me – is that *whatever* they are, God is right beside us all the way.

'Dixons *don't* know that yet. And that's such a shame. Which is why it's so important that we keep on praying that one day they will.'

Six

Up in his bedroom, Clyde sat at his desk. He'd been there all evening.

Every so often, he reached round behind his head and placed his left hand on the back of his neck. The skin of his palm felt cool against it. It soothed the heat in his neck, which had been quite badly sunburnt from hanging around near the shopping centre. He'd spent almost the whole day there, watching Lizzi create a new pavement picture. It had been hot. Several times, he'd thought he should probably find some shade. But instead, he'd stayed where he was. He hadn't wanted to miss seeing Lizzi work. Not for a second.

Now it was Clyde's turn to draw. The top of his desk was a mess of rubber dust. He could see the picture he wanted to create quite clearly inside his head, but getting it onto the paper in front of him – exactly as it was in his mind, *exactly* right – was hard. For a long while, the picture didn't grow and the stump of his rubber got smaller and smaller.

Lizzi had told Clyde to people-watch. That's where he'd find stories, she'd said, and it was stories that gave you ideas.

The most interesting story Clyde had found that day was Lizzi herself. When she'd told Clyde that she hadn't any idea whether or not one or other of her parents was an artist, he'd asked, 'How? How can you not know?'

She'd looked at him mischievously. 'I don't think I'm going to tell you,' she answered.

'Why, though? Why not?'

'Because where's the fun in that? If you know

everything about a person straight away, there's no mystery, is there? But what you *don't* know – what you can only guess at – now that's much more exciting! It's what you *don't* know that gets your imagination moving. Just think of all the different stories you might come up with while you're trying to guess at the truth!'

Clyde's drawing was of a tree. It had a thick, gnarled trunk like an ancient oak. Clyde had spent ages working on the patterns and ridges and splits in the bark. At the trunk top, he'd drawn branch upon branch. They twisted and pushed and thrust their way upwards and outwards.

But that's where the realistic image of a tree came to an end. Clyde's tree had sprouted, but not into leaves. Instead, the branches were hung with question marks. For Clyde, each question mark stood for someone's untold story; what you didn't know, but were desperate to discover; the imagined story you might come up with while you were trying to guess at the truth – just as Lizzi had said.

There was a tap on Clyde's bedroom door.

'Are you all right in there?' asked his mum. 'You've been ever so quiet this evening.'

Clyde wanted to be left alone. 'I'm fine,' he muttered.

'Can I come in?'

'I'm fine, Mum,' he said again. 'I'll be down in a bit.'

'It'll be *bedtime* in a bit,' his mum replied. 'Never mind yours. *Mine*!'

Clyde raised his eyes. He looked back at his question mark tree. It was almost finished. The outlines, at least. He wanted to paint it, but there wasn't time for that tonight. In any case, he wasn't sure how much paint he had left. He'd bought himself a box of watercolours with some money he'd been given last Christmas, but he'd used them a lot already. He hoped he'd have enough.

He wanted the picture to be finished by next weekend. That's when he'd see Lizzi again. He'd had an idea – a stupid idea, he kept telling himself, but it was something he wanted to do anyway. Clyde never liked anyone to see his paintings. But he wanted to show Lizzi this one. He wanted to know what she'd think of it, just like *she'd* wanted to hear what he thought of *her* pictures. Of course, she'd know the painting was Clyde's but he reckoned she'd be honest anyway. She'd be honest because he'd ask her to be.

'Clyde?' His mum still hovered outside his door.

He snatched up the drawing, twisted on his chair and slid it away out of sight under the bed.

'What d'you want, Mum?' he answered, irritated.

The door opened just enough for his mum to peer around. 'What have you been doing in here all evening?'

'Nothing,' Clyde said. 'What is it?'

His mum held out a card. 'I just want you to sign this.'

Clyde looked at her blankly.

'Ashley's birthday card,' his mum said. 'Don't tell me you've forgotten it's her birthday tomorrow.'

Clyde had. He'd forgotten it completely.

His mum shook her head. 'I only reminded you yesterday. You won't have bought her a present, then.'

'No,' Clyde grunted. 'I haven't got any money anyway.'

'Well, I wish you'd said,' sighed his mum. 'I could have got you something to give her. Your dad's not going to be very happy, is he?'

'Why?' Clyde snapped. 'It's not *his* birthday I've forgotten.'

'Oh, you know what I mean!' His mum pressed

a hand to her forehead. 'Why isn't anything ever straightforward in this house?'

Straightforward didn't seem to exist in the Bicton family. There was always a problem somewhere; an argument brewing.

Clyde signed the card, then went down to the kitchen. He was hungry. He grabbed a handful of biscuits and started back upstairs. As he did so, his dad and Ashley came out of the lounge.

'Aha!' said Rob. 'The vanishing Clyde reappears!' He glanced at the biscuits in his son's hands. 'I knew you'd turn up when you were hungry.'

Clyde was half way up the stairs when his dad's voice stopped him again.

'And where have you been all day? Your mate Kevin's been round here a couple of times looking for you.'

Clyde shrugged. 'It's 'cos he hasn't got a mobile. Kevin never knows where anyone is.'

'So, where have you been?' his dad persisted. 'We've hardly seen you.'

'Just out,' Clyde said. He didn't want his dad to know he'd been watching Lizzi draw her pavement pictures. He especially didn't want to tell him in front of Ashley.

'Well, make sure you don't disappear off tomorrow after school,' his dad said. 'It's Ashley's birthday, remember. I thought we'd try and do something.'

Clyde nodded and once again went to go back to his room. This time it was Ashley's voice that stopped him.

'Don't worry, he won't disappear off tomorrow, Dad. Lizzi's only working weekends.'

Clyde shot Ashley a look.

'Oh, yeah, I saw you,' Ashley said breezily. 'But you were so ...' – she paused slightly to emphasise the word – '...

involved in Lizzi's drawing, you didn't notice me.'

'What drawing?' asked Rob. 'What are you on about?'

'It's where Clyde's been all day,' replied Ashley. 'Down at the shopping centre watching Lizzi Brewer scribble on the pavement.'

'Lizzi Brewer?' Their dad raised a questioning eyebrow.

'She's the girl I told you about, remember?' Ashley continued. 'She's raising money to go to a summer school of art in Paris.'

'That's it!' said their dad, clicking his fingers as he remembered. 'Graffiti. She makes a mess everywhere or something, doesn't she?'

Ashley smirked. 'Clyde obviously doesn't think it's a mess. He was watching for ages.'

'It's *not* a mess, that's why,' Clyde muttered.

'Actually, Dad, you're right, it is,' said Ashley. 'A mess, I mean. It's like I said before, everyone thinks Lizzi Brewer's SO clever, but she's not.'

Ashley was doing it on purpose. Deliberately winding Clyde up. Clyde knew he ought to just walk away; get back to his room. But he'd made friends with Lizzi. He loved her pavement art. And she *was* good, she was *really* good. He couldn't stand there and listen to Ashley bad-mouthing her without trying to stick up for her.

'But she *is* clever,' he hissed.

Ashley shook her head. 'Says someone who knows nothing about art.'

'She is clever, Dad,' Clyde said again. 'Everyone says so. Everyone who's seen her pictures. Everyone who's been down the shopping centre.' A thought struck him and his eyes lit up. 'We could go down there now! I could show you! The pictures are still there on the walkway. You'll be able to see for yourself.

They're brilliant! They're really brilliant!'

Ashley sniggered. And as fast as Clyde's eyes had lit up, the gleam in them faded again. Just the look on his dad's face told him he had no interest in seeing Lizzi's drawings.

'Nah,' Rob said. 'I'm not into graffiti. Anyway, if Ashley says the girl's work's rubbish, then that's good enough for me.'

Clyde suddenly couldn't keep his temper.

'Why do you always do that, Dad?' he burst out. 'Why do you always side with *her*?'

Rob frowned at him. 'What's that supposed to mean?' he demanded. There was a warning in his voice. 'I didn't think there were sides to take, Clyde. We were talking about graffiti.'

'What's going on?' Cathy appeared on the upstairs landing.

'Ashley's jealous, that's what's going on!' Clyde growled. 'She knows Lizzi's art's way, *way* better than hers! She knows she'll never even be a *quarter* as good! That's why she says it's rubbish. Because she knows she can't do it!'

'That is enough, Clyde!' Cathy cut in before Rob had the chance. 'You'd better get back to your room now.'

Clyde glared at her. 'Yeah,' he muttered. 'And maybe I'll just stay there forever and ever and *never* come out *ever* again!'

He stormed back up the remaining stairs slamming his bedroom door shut. If only it had a lock. Then he could keep everyone out. All day every day.

Every day. All day.

Seven

Clyde wasn't in the room when Ashley unwrapped her birthday presents. He spotted them spread out on the sofa on his way out to school. There were a few books and DVDs. But most of the presents looked like art materials: large and small sketchpads, watercolour and oil paints, pencils and pastels. They would have been his dad's idea for sure. Ashley was still his 'little artist' just the way she was when she was a small child. And now that she was doing so well in art at Bruford Secondary School, he clearly wanted to show that he was right behind her; that he believed in her ability, admired her talent and wanted to do everything he could to help and encourage her.

Would his dad do that for him, Clyde wondered? If he knew how much Clyde had grown to love doing art at school, would he believe in him, too?

'Don't forget, Clyde.' His mum stood behind him. 'Straight back here after school. We'll probably go out for a pizza or something and then maybe to the cinema. And here.' She thrust a five pound note into his hands. 'Get a present for Ashley on your way home.'

Clyde looked down at the money sullenly. 'Like what?'

'I don't know. What about a big box of chocolates? She'll like that.'

Clyde nodded; headed for the front door.

'Straight back after school, Clyde,' his mum repeated. 'Please.'

Sometimes Clyde felt sorry for his mum. She was the peacemaker in the house, the one who always tried to stop the quarrels before they started; to sort them out if they were already under way. She always looked tired, Clyde thought. Half the time she seemed nervous. On edge.

Other times Clyde was angry with her. She tried to keep the peace, yes, but she didn't stick up for him. Not really. Clyde's mum knew that he could draw. His teacher had praised him for it at the last two parents' evenings. Clyde's dad hadn't been able to get to them because of work. But when he'd asked how they'd gone, all his mum had said was, 'Fine. Better at some things than others, aren't you, Clyde, but on the whole fine.'

Of course, she'd skated over the bad comments, too, so as not to set Clyde's dad off nagging again. But it would have meant so much to Clyde – the *world* to him – if she could just have told his dad that as far as his artwork went, he was top of the class. Even when it was mentioned in his school reports, she played it down.

Clyde had once asked her why; why what he did wasn't as important as what Ashley did.

'Of course it's as important!' his mum had said. 'It's just – well, your dad sees Ashley as the artist in the family and he might think you're trying to compete with her or something. You know how funny he gets. If only it was science you were good at, eh, Clyde? Ashley hates science so it wouldn't matter.'

Why did it matter anyway, Clyde wondered? Why wasn't there room for two artists in the Bicton family?

And if there was only room for one, why couldn't it be him?

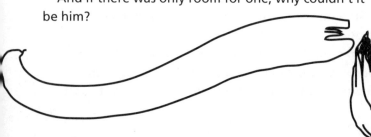

Dave had lost his enthusiasm for the cycle track. He hadn't even been back to the park since Dixons had ruined his and Paul's sketch.

He'd read the Bible verse Greg had given him from Jeremiah. He'd prayed for Dixons the way Greg had told him to. But he hadn't been back. He still wished he never had to see a Dixons boy ever again.

At school, the others in the Topz Gang tried to cheer him up.

'Trouble is, you can't avoid them,' said Benny. 'It's not like we haven't tried.'

'Then maybe I need to try harder,' grumbled Dave.

'Dad says that if we ignore them, then one day they'll get bored with picking on us,' said Sarah. 'And when they do, they'll leave us alone.'

'But when will that be, Sarah?' Dave answered snappily. 'It's been years already and they're still doing it.'

'At least they don't go to the same school as us any more,' said John. 'It was worse when they did.'

'Was it?' mumbled Dave. 'It doesn't feel like it.'

'You're not coming to the park after school, then?' said Danny. 'I brought my football.'

Dave shook his head. 'I'm never going back to the park,' he said. 'I know I'll end up seeing them around all over the place anyway, but I'm never going back to the park.'

Paul's face fell. 'But what about the cycle track? We had some really good ideas. We need to draw them again and send them in. And when it's built it's going to be amazing! You know it is! If you don't ever go to the park, how will you be able to use it?'

'None of us'll be able to use it, Paul,' Dave replied. 'Don't you get it? Dixons will *always* be there. *Always.* Just like they're *always* everywhere.'

When school was over, Dave ambled by himself out through the main gates.

'Dave, wait!'

Paul ran across the playground to catch him up.
'I know you don't want to put in any ideas for the cycle track, but *I* still do,' he puffed. 'I wanna try to draw something out tonight. The deadline for getting it in's quite soon. I don't wanna miss it.'

Dave nodded. 'Fine,' he said. 'You can use any of the ideas I came up with. I don't really care.'

'Thanks,' said Paul. 'Only I haven't got any paper. Not decent paper so it all looks really professional.'

'I don't think anyone expects it to be professional-looking, Paul,' Dave answered. 'It's a competition for kids. It doesn't matter what you draw it on.'

'That's not what you thought before. You wanted it to look really good. That's why you borrowed your dad's sketchpad.'

'Yeah,' Dave grunted, 'and look what happened to that.'

Paul raised his eyes. 'Look, just stop being so grumpy, Dave! Come to The Art Shop with me. I'm going there now.'

Dave looked at him. 'The Art Shop? What do you want from The Art Shop?'

'Uh – paper!' said Paul. 'Haven't you been listening?'

'You can get pads of paper from the corner shop.'

'Yes, but like I say, I want *good* paper. Proper arty paper. So it looks like I've taken lots of trouble. And we can talk about the cycle track on the way. I can't remember all the ideas we had, you know what I'm like. Sometimes I wish my glasses had memory cells. In fact, one day I'm going to *invent* a pair of glasses with memory cells.'

Dave sighed. 'OK,' he said, 'I'll come. But then I'm going home. You're not gonna persuade me to do this with you, so don't try.'

'I wasn't going to,' Paul said.

'No,' Dave replied. 'Of course you weren't.'

As they crossed the walkway leading to the shopping centre, they paused to admire Lizzi's pictures. There had been no rain and the pastel drawings from the weekend still decorated the paving slabs. They were just a little faded and smudged from where footsteps had cut across them or the street-sweeping machine had brushed a little too close. The lady in the green armchair; further away a dragon covered in scales, also green in colour, and with a long, long tail that curled its way around the outer edge of the walkway.

'You should get *her* to draw the cycle track,' said Dave. 'The girl that drew these. She'd make it look incredible.'

'She would,' agreed Paul. 'But if I've got the right paper, I reckon I can make it look pretty incredible, too. Although,' he added pointedly, '*not* as incredible as if you'd helped me.'

Dave smiled. It was the first time he'd smiled all day. For several days in fact.

'Not falling for it, Paul,' he said.

'Don't know what you mean,' his friend grinned.

'Yes, you do. I'm not having anything to do with the cycle track and that's that.'

'Fine by me,' answered Paul. 'Like I say, all I really need is the right paper.'

The two boys walked on through the shopping centre until they reached The Art Shop. Neither of them had ever been inside. It was a place for people who were serious about art. There were shelves and shelves of paper and paints, brushes and crayons and pencils. There were displays of equipment like easels and adjustable stools. And there were all sorts of pictures stacked together in racks, and rolled-up posters clustered in baskets.

Paul picked up a pad that looked the same sort of size as the one Dave had borrowed from his dad.

'What d'you think?' he asked.

Dave nodded. 'It's paper, Paul. It'll do.'

'Yeah, but is it professional-looking enough?'

A smartly dressed lady behind the counter eyed them both a little suspiciously. The Topz boys did look as though they'd be more at home in a sweet shop than an art shop.

'Do you need any help?' she asked.

'No, thanks, I just want to buy this, please,' said Paul.

He had his back to Dave as he stood at the counter and fished out his money. So he didn't see what Dave saw through the shop window.

Dave's eyes widened. He stared through the glass in disbelief.

Peering in from outside was a boy. A Dixons boy. Clyde.

There were reflections in the big window. Clyde cupped his hands around his eyes to see in better. He didn't spot Dave and Paul. He looked to the right where there were some boxes of watercolour paints; screwed up his eyes to try to see.

He didn't even notice the two boys when he pushed open the shop door and stepped inside. He was too interested in one particular shelf of paints.

The lady serving Paul looked up. Keeping half an eye on Clyde, she handed Paul his change and slipped the pad of paper he'd just bought into a carrier bag.

Paul turned. Before he even had a chance to follow Dave's gaze, Dave said loudly, 'You'd better hold on to that tightly, Paul. There's a Dixon in the shop.'

Clyde spun round. He stared at Dave – the very last person in the world he would have expected to bump into in The Art Shop.

Dave glowered back at him. 'What did I say, Paul?' he muttered. 'Dixons! You can't get away from them. They're *always everywhere!*'

Eight

'I was looking for you.'

Clyde stood in front of Lizzi. She sat on the bench outside the baker's, a large takeaway cup of coffee in one hand.

'I waited by your pictures. I thought you'd be there.'

'*I* thought I'd be there, too,' said Lizzi. 'That was the plan. First thing Saturday morning, set myself up and try and gather a crowd. There's rain coming in later so I wanted to start early.'

'So what happened?'

Lizzi sighed. 'My confidence, Clyde, that's what.' She tossed her head. 'Boof! Suddenly, away it flew out of the window.'

Clyde made a face. 'What are you talking about? You've got loads of confidence. Your pictures are awesome! You know they are.'

Lizzi glanced up at him. She patted the bench beside her.

'Sit,' she said. 'Unless you want to go grab yourself a doughnut or five.'

Clyde shook his head and sat down.

Lizzi raised her eyebrows. 'Seriously? No doughnuts?'

'Seriously,' Clyde grunted. 'No money.'

'Hah!' Lizzi laughed. 'I know *that* feeling.'

'So why aren't you out there drawing?' Clyde asked. 'People give you money when they see you draw.'

Lizzi dropped her gaze. She seemed different from when Clyde had last seen her. Quieter; thoughtful.

'What's wrong?' he said. 'Are you sad?'

'Not sad exactly,' Lizzi began. 'I just … well, I wanted to do something different today.'

'Different how?'

'I think if you do too much of the same thing, people get bored.'

'The pavement pictures, you mean?' said Clyde. 'People could *never* get bored with them.'

'You'd be surprised,' Lizzi answered. 'Anyway, bored or not, I wanted to try doing something that people could take away with them rather than just seeing it sprawled on the pavement. End up with something worthwhile for their money.'

'Something like …?'

'Portraits.'

Admiration glowed instantly in Clyde's eyes. 'You can do portraits, too?'

'Not serious portraits,' Lizzi smiled. 'Caricatures. You know what a caricature is?'

'I think so,' said Clyde. 'Sort of like a cartoon version of someone.'

'Yeah,' Lizzi nodded. 'I mean, I can do them. I know I can.'

Clyde held up his hands. 'So what's stopping you?'

Lizzi dropped her head; took a sip of coffee. 'Me,' she said. 'And, yes, I suppose I am sad.'

'What for?' Clyde frowned.

Lizzi was silent for a moment. Then, 'I don't know why I'm telling you but … it's my birthday today,' she said.

'Huh!' said Clyde, flatly. 'That's funny. It was Ashley's birthday a few days ago, too.'

'Yes, I know. She talked about it at school. How her dad had bought her all this art stuff. How he really believed in her.'

Clyde narrowed his eyes; peered at Lizzi. 'What's going on?' he asked. 'Has she been mean to you?'

The shopping centre had begun to fill up. People ambled past or strode out more briskly. It was noisy now.

Lizzi glanced back at him. 'Tell you what, d'you fancy a walk?' she said. 'It's getting really busy in here.'

'A walk?'

'Yeah. You know, it's where you move your legs backwards and forwards and end up somewhere else.'

'Funny,' muttered Clyde.

Lizzi's holdall sat on the ground at her feet. He nodded towards it.

'But you've got your bag,' he said. 'It'll mean lugging it around.'

Lizzi shrugged. 'My bag, my lugging. I'm not bothered.' She finished her coffee; dropped the cup into the bin beside the bench. 'Shall we go?'

They wandered in amongst the shops and the shoppers, peeping into windows, not saying much.

At one point, an elderly lady stopped them.

'You're the girl who's been drawing those pictures, aren't you?' she beamed. 'They're just wonderful, you know. I hope you're going to do some more. We need things like that in Holly Hill. Brightens up the place.'

'You see?' said Clyde as they walked on. 'People love what you do. Have you got your confidence back now?'

With the shopping centre behind them, they turned off and made their way up through the industrial estate. As it was Saturday, the road was quiet. They sat down on the stretch of grass behind the supermarket. They could hear car doors being slammed; the clatter of shopping trolleys.

'You still haven't told me why you're sad,' Clyde said.

'It's your birthday. You should be happy.'

Lizzi gazed into the distance. Somewhere a baby was crying.

'I'm always sad on my birthday,' she murmured.

'But why?' Clyde asked.

Lizzi turned to look at him. 'You've got a mum and a dad, haven't you?' she said quietly. 'A real mum and dad?'

'Yeah. You know I have.'

Lizzi nodded. 'That's the thing you see … I haven't.'

Clyde blinked at her. 'What, so you mean … they're dead?'

'No, they're not dead. I'm pretty sure they're not dead anyway. I think I'd know if they were.' She hesitated. 'I'm adopted, Clyde.'

'Right.' Clyde wasn't sure what to say. He hadn't expected that. Lizzi had left him with questions about her. Her story was one of the question marks on the tree he'd drawn. But it had never occurred to him that this was how the story went.

'How long?' he asked.

'Oh, my whole life,' said Lizzi. 'I was just a baby.'

'That's why you don't know if your parents are artists.'

'Uh-huh. Haven't the faintest clue. I mean, don't get me wrong, my adoptive parents are great and wonderful and I love them. I really do love them.' She paused; fiddled with her long, red plait. 'But on my birthday, I get sad. Can't help it. I always end up wondering why they didn't want me, my real parents. Why they gave me away.'

'Have you ever tried to find them?' Clyde asked.

'No.'

'Will you?'

'Maybe. Some day. If they don't find me first.'

Clyde shifted on the grass. 'Why do you say that? D'you think they're looking?'

'I have no idea, Clyde.' Lizzi sounded a little impatient. As if she'd had enough of the conversation. 'I'll tell you what I *think*, shall I?' She smiled again. 'You see, I *think* that one of my parents *is* an artist. A good one, too. And I *think* it's my mum. I think that's where I get all of this from. From my mum.

'And I *think* we have similar styles,' Lizzi went on. She seemed almost excited. 'I mean if I ever saw a picture that my mum – my real mum – had painted, I'd *know* it was hers. I'd just know – because it would be something like a painting *I* would have done. And if my mum ever saw one of *my* pictures, it would be the same thing. She'd know! She'd know that that little baby she'd given away all those years ago had created it.'

Lizzi stopped talking for a moment; stretched out her legs, wriggled her toes in their flip-flops.

'That's mostly why I wanted to go to Paris,' she added. 'To the summer school. If my mum's an artist anywhere, it'll be in Paris, I know it will. And if I can find her paintings, then maybe I'll be able to find her.'

They sat in silence for a while. A ginger cat strolled past. It rubbed itself against Lizzi's bag, but when she went to stroke it, it just skittered away.

Clyde stared down at his hands. He traced the lines in the palm of one with the thumb of the other. The tree picture he'd drawn was folded up and tucked into his pocket. He wanted to show Lizzi. He wanted to be brave enough.

'Is that why you didn't have any confidence today?' he asked. 'Because you've been thinking about your mum and dad not wanting you?'

Lizzi sighed. 'I suppose. Don't know, really. Just one of those days.'

Clyde took a deep breath. 'I like doing art stuff at school,' he said. 'I told you that, didn't I? It's the *only* thing I like. And I'm not saying that I'm good at it or anything, because I don't know that I am, but … I think I want to be an artist one day.'

He screwed up his face; dug his fingernails into his palms. It sounded so stupid when he said it out loud.

'I do,' he added in a whisper. 'I think I want to be an artist.'

Lizzi looked at him. 'Wow! You *and* Ashley, eh? And what do your parents make of that? I reckon they're either *really* pleased and supportive, or *really* worried that neither of you will ever settle down and get a proper job!'

It was Clyde's turn to look sad. 'Dad supports Ashley,' he said. 'He's proud of her. You can see it all over his face.'

Lizzi frowned. 'I bet he's proud of you, too. He probably just finds it harder to show it – I dunno, because you're a boy or something.'

'No.' Clyde reached into his pocket. He pulled out the folded up picture. 'But it's not going to stop me doing what I want.'

'What's that?' Lizzi nodded towards the paper in Clyde's hand.

'I never think anything I do is any good,' Clyde mumbled. 'I mean, my teacher likes my artwork. He says nice things about it. It's the *only* thing he says nice things about because I'm rubbish at everything else. I think that's all my dad sees all the time. The rubbish bit. It's like …' He stopped; thought carefully about what he wanted to say. 'It's like Dad can *see* Ashley. But he can't see me.

Not really. And because he can't see *me*, somehow I can't see *him*.'

He looked up at Lizzi. 'I'm sorry for you and everything. I can't imagine what that must be like – knowing that your parents gave you away. But sometimes when I'm around Dad, I end up feeling so stupid and useless that d'you know what I wish? I wish he'd given *me* away. Then I might have ended up with a family that believed in me.'

A deep frown dug itself into Lizzi's forehead. 'That's a terrible thing to say, Clyde,' she said.

'I know,' Clyde murmured.

Lizzi hugged her knees into her chest. 'What's on the paper?' she asked again.

Slowly Clyde began to unfold it. 'I never show anyone my pictures. Not the ones I do at home. I hide them all away because I'm like you are today. I've got no confidence. Only I'm like it all the time.'

He paused; swallowed. 'But I did this one after you told me about stories. Stories that make up people; that give you ideas. It's the picture that came into my head. And it's not properly finished because I ran out of paint and I looked at the prices in the shop and I couldn't afford any more. And it's a shame because if it was finished then you might think it was better. But I want to show you anyway. Because if you tell me it's no good, then I'll know Dad's right not to believe in me. But if you tell me it's OK – well, I'll know he's wrong. And then maybe I can start believing in myself.'

Lizzi gazed at him. 'And what makes you think I know anything about what's good or bad in art?'

'Because you're clever,' muttered Clyde, 'and you know what you like.'

Lizzi nodded. 'And what makes you think I'll tell you the truth?'

Clyde looked down at the paper in his hands. He shrugged. 'Because you want other people to tell you the truth about *your* pictures.'

Carefully, he finished smoothing the creases.

Then he held the drawing out to Lizzi.

Nine

R U hiding?

Dave glanced at his phone. The text that had just arrived was from Paul.

He texted back: *No.*

Another text from Paul bleeped in: *So Y weren't U at youth club?*

Dave raised his eyes; punched in a reply: *Just wasn't.*

Paul replied: *It's half term. U can't hide 4ever.*

Dave hated texting. He went to his contacts list, found Paul and jabbed 'call'.

'Paul,' he said, 'you know I don't like texting. It gives me cramp in my thumb. And I'm not hiding.'

'Then why weren't you at youth club?' Paul asked. 'You're always at youth club.'

'Well, I wasn't there yesterday, so obviously not.'

'But *why* not?'

'Why does it matter?'

'Because,' said Paul, 'if it's got anything to do with avoiding Dixons, I've got a message for you from Greg.'

'What?'

'Greg asked where you were, so I told him I didn't know – which I didn't. But I said that wherever you were, the reason you weren't at youth club was probably because you didn't want to see any of the Dixons Gang ever again. By the way, none of them were there last night, so you'd have been quite safe.'

Paul gabbled on, hardly pausing for breath.

'Greg asked if you were still having trouble with them and I said, "Well, *you* know Dixons. Even if they're not *actually* causing trouble at any one moment, you can't help sort of waiting for them to start." I told Greg I thought that was what you were doing – waiting for them to start something again. I mean, from that point of view hiding away makes sense. Tons of sense. After all, the best way to avoid getting picked on is to avoid the pickers, I suppose. "Trouble is," I said to Greg, "we all live in Holly Hill, and if Dave's planning to avoid Dixons by not going to the park, or the shopping centre, or youth club – and maybe even church, because you have to walk fairly close to the shopping centre to get to it – then that only really leaves school. And what kind of fun is he going to have if the only place he ever goes any more is school? Not much, that's what. So," I said to Greg, "what are we going to do about it?"'

Silence.

Paul had stopped talking and Dave was so stunned that his friend had even had this conversation with Greg, he didn't know what to say.

'Erm … hello?'

'Hello,' Dave replied flatly.

'Oh, that's good,' said Paul cheerfully. 'I thought we'd got cut off and I was going to have to ring you back and say *all* of that all over again.'

'No!' answered Dave quickly. 'I heard you! Please don't say it all over again!'

'Anyway,' and once more Paul was off, 'the thing is Greg said some really useful stuff and I told him I'd pass it on, so here I go – passing it on. Are you ready?'

Dave sighed. 'Yeah.' Paul would tell him, ready or not.

'The first thing he said was that no one should put up with someone else being horrible to them or bullying them. Not ever. So he said that if you needed to, you could go and talk to him about it again. Or you could talk to your parents. He said if Dixons were making you feel *that* bad, then something would have to be done about it. So Greg said to tell you that you're not on your own dealing with it. That's good to know, isn't it?'

'I *know* I'm not on my own,' Dave muttered. 'And if there was anything to talk about, then I'd talk about it. It's really not that it's *that* bad. And it's not even like it's just me, is it? They pick on all of us. I guess it's just Dixons. They've never liked us and I don't suppose they ever will. But why would *anyone* want to go *anywhere* they're almost bound to see someone who's going to wind them up and be nasty? What's the point? I mean who would do that?'

'Jesus would!' said Paul excitedly. 'Jesus *did*!'

Dave listened as Paul chattered on about everything Greg had said. How Jesus didn't run away from people or avoid them; He'd come to earth to teach people about God and to show them how God wanted them to live; to let them know that God loved them and how they could be His friends. That was Jesus' purpose and He carried it out, even when people turned against Him; even as they put Him to death.

'Greg gave me these verses,' Paul added. 'Verses 14 to 16 from Matthew 5: *"You are like light for the whole world ... No one lights a lamp and puts it under a bowl; instead he puts it on the lampstand, where it gives light for everyone in the house. In the same way your light must shine before people, so that they will see the good things you do and praise your Father in heaven."*

'Greg says it's up to us who are Jesus' friends right now to keep telling people about God; to keep letting them know how much He loves them and wants to be *their* Friend. He says we can do that by talking about God, but we can also do it by the way we behave and live our lives. People might not seem interested – they might not even like us for it – but if we can show God to them just by being around, at least they might start to think about Him. And if they see how much He means to us, then maybe one day, He might mean that much to them, too. But,' Paul went on, 'that's only going to happen, Greg says, if we're out there being around other people.

'We need to be out and about in Holly Hill, Dave. In the park, at the shops. Just by doing that we can remind Dixons that God's there.'

That all made sense. A lot of sense. But then, whatever the situation, what Greg said *always* made sense. Not just to Dave; to everyone he spoke to. Greg was good at finding the right words and knowing when was the right time to use them. He seemed to be able to show God to everyone all the time.

If Dave hid himself away, how could *he* do that? How could *he* show God to anyone? It would be like Jesus said – hiding his lamp under a bowl and leaving the rest of the house in darkness.

And God's love and forgiveness were too important to keep to himself.

Dave flipped open his Bible. Jesus had more to say about showing God to other people; teaching them about Him: *'Go, then, to all peoples everywhere and make them my disciples ... and teach them to obey everything I have commanded you. And I will be with you always, to the end of the age'* (Matthew 28, verses 19–20).

Dave read the words: Jesus' instructions. They explained exactly what Jesus wanted His friends to do.

Jesus didn't add, 'But only teach the people who you like and who are nice to you,' or, 'If you really don't feel like it, don't bother.'

He just said: 'Do it.'

I'm not always very good at following instructions, am I, God?

Dave read the verses from Matthew over again.

Especially when they're hard instructions. I put off doing hard homework all the time. Then I have to do it all in a rush so that I can still give it in on time but it ends up not being very good. And sometimes I just get it plain wrong. A bit like trying to avoid bumping into Dixons, I suppose. Only that's not just wrong, that's silly.

*It's not easy, God, thinking of yourself as a 'light for the whole world'. Especially when you're in a bad mood. When I'm in a bad mood, all I want to do is be by myself. I can't be bothered with anyone much, not even Topz. So trying to be bothered with Dixons feels like – well – impossible. I don't **want** to be bothered with them. I don't **want** to keep setting myself up as a target for them.*

*But then like Greg says, Jesus was a target, too. There were people who hated Him, but that didn't stop Him doing the work You wanted Him to do. So I suppose I can't really let it stop me either. And I know I'm not on my own, God. I've got Topz and I've got Greg and I've got Mum and Dad. And **You'll** be with me wherever I am, because that's Your promise, isn't it?*

So could You please help me, God? If You want me to be a lamp around Holly Hill, please could You help me to shine brightly enough to make a difference. Not just to Dixons, but wherever I am and whoever I'm with. And when my light goes out – sorry, God, but I know it will because I get in bad moods, sometimes – please switch it back on again.

I want to try to be like Jesus, God. I want to be a lamp that never goes out.

Ten

Clyde didn't hear the doorbell ring. He was up in his bedroom playing music.

Ashley answered it. She was surprised when she opened the door.

'Hi, Ashley, is Clyde around?' It was Lizzi.

'Erm …' Ashley hesitated. Why would Lizzi Brewer be after Clyde?

'It's just I said I'd drop by with some information for him,' Lizzi added.

Ashley stared at her. 'What about?'

'Just an art week for kids that's going to happen at Bruford in the summer holidays. Clyde's just the right age. The information's going to primary schools after half-term, but that's only a week away, so I thought there's no harm in telling him about it now.'

Ashley made a face. 'And why would Clyde want to go on an art week?' she asked. 'Come to think of it, why would an art week want Clyde?'

Lizzi gave her a hard look. 'I tell you what, Ashley,' she said, 'if you ever actually looked at his art, I think you'd know why.'

Ashley nodded; just slightly. 'So if the information's not going out until after half-term, how come *you* know so much about it?'

'Because I've been asked to help out. It fits in well actually,' Lizzi added breezily. 'It's just before I go to Paris and I'm going to get paid.' She paused; glanced around Ashley into the hall. 'So is Clyde here?'

Ashley didn't even blink. 'No, he's not.'

'OK,' Lizzi smiled, 'then could you make sure he

gets this?' She held out a flier. Ashley took it. 'All the details are on there.'

Lizzi turned to go but almost immediately looked back. 'You should encourage Clyde to have a go, Ashley,' she said. 'It'd be good for him. I reckon he's got a lot of potential.'

Ashley closed the front door. She leaned against it as she scanned the information Lizzi had left.

There were a limited number of places available for the art week, so children from the local primary schools would be selected to take part. They were asked to submit a painting; a piece of work they had already finished or a new picture painted specially. The deadline for getting artwork in was 25 June. The two art teachers at Bruford who would run the week would then choose their favourite pictures, and the children who had painted them would be invited to attend.

Ashley read all this. She shook her head and pursed her lips.

Clyde wasn't an artist. He was just a stupid boy trying to copy his big sister. And Lizzi was stupid, too, if she thought any different.

Ashley wandered through to the kitchen. She paused by the bin next to the sink and glanced towards the door. Then she scrunched the flier into a ball and dropped it in.

Clyde lay on his bed with his eyes closed. He tried to concentrate. He needed an idea for a picture but there was nothing in his head. Nothing any good at least.

He couldn't paint something ordinary. Not for this picture; that wouldn't be good enough.

This idea had to be amazing. It had to stand out.

And he only had one chance to get it right.

As hard as Clyde tried to focus, his mind kept drifting back to Saturday morning. He'd sat with Lizzi on the grass near the supermarket. He'd shown her his picture of the question mark tree.

Lizzi had looked at it for a long time. She hadn't said much but she'd told him she liked it. She liked it a lot. And Clyde had believed her.

'Do you understand it, though?' Clyde had asked. 'It's no good if it doesn't make sense.'

'I think everyone makes sense of the things they see and the things they hear in their own way,' Lizzi replied. 'Sometimes giving a picture a title helps. I'd guess ...' she gazed at the tree thoughtfully. 'Looking at this, I'd guess that there are a lot of things you want to know, and there are lots of things to *be* known. To be found out. I don't think this is a sad picture, though,' she added. 'It doesn't feel sad – as if you know there are secrets, bad secrets maybe, and you need to know the truth. It feels more like ... an *expectant* picture. You know, like there's so much out there to discover.'

Clyde nodded. 'I've got a title,' he said. 'I mean, I've only just thought of it but I think it's the right one. It says the right thing. To me anyway. Do you want to hear it?'

'Go on, then.'

'*The Story Tree*,' he murmured. He felt self-conscious saying it out loud. 'I think I'd like to call it *The Story Tree*.'

Instantly, Lizzi beamed. 'I *love* that!' she cried. 'And do you know what I'd do if it was *my* picture and I had it in an exhibition? I'd have paper and pens there and

I'd ask people who looked at it to write a bit of their own personal story – just a tiny piece that they didn't mind sharing – and then leave it by the picture for other people to read. Then those stories would become a part of the exhibition.'

'I told you you were clever,' Clyde muttered. 'I'd never have thought of that.'

Lizzi nudged him with her elbow. 'Of course you would! You just need a little help. A little bit of pointing in the right direction. Everyone does. I've been studying art, remember? I'm *supposed* to have ideas like that. Be kind of alarming if I didn't! In fact ...'

Lizzi broke off. A thought had struck her. She looked at Clyde, eyes narrowed, head on one side.

'In fact ... well, there's going to be an art week at Bruford. It'd be perfect for you!'

Clyde raised his eyebrows. 'In case you haven't noticed, I'm not old enough to go to Bruford.'

'I know that, silly,' she laughed. 'There's going to be an art week at Bruford in the summer holidays for kids like *you*. Kids who really love painting and drawing and want to get better. I'm helping out with it. The information's being sent out to primary schools after half-term.'

Lizzi expected Clyde's face to light up, but it did the opposite.

He shook his head. 'No, I could never do anything like that.'

'Yes, you could!' Lizzi said. 'And it would be so good for you! Mr Keller's an amazing art teacher and so is Miss Pendleton. They're going to run it together. You'd learn loads ... Oh ...'

That's when she remembered.

'There's just one thing, but you mustn't let it put you off.'

Clyde frowned. 'What?'

'Well … you have to paint to get picked …'

Stretched out on his bed, Clyde opened his eyes. He'd gone over and over the conversation he'd had with Lizzi. He tried to stop thinking about it; to get his brain to focus on coming up with ideas for a picture that might land him a place on the Bruford art week. But he couldn't. Even listening to music didn't help.

Lizzi was the first person who'd ever seemed to believe in him. It was such an incredible feeling – and Clyde didn't want to let it go.

He sat up suddenly, put out his hand and snapped off the music. He could go out, he thought. Lizzi had told him that stories were everywhere, so the best place to be was out of the house.

He ran downstairs; slipped on his trainers just as his dad came in from work.

'Where are you off to, Clyde?' he asked.

'Not sure,' Clyde shrugged. 'Park, I think.'

'And what have you been doing all day? Anything useful?'

Clyde's dad didn't look at his son. He bent down to untie his shoelaces. He took off his jacket and hung it on the hook by the door. He glanced through to the kitchen.

Clyde watched him. He would love to have told his dad what he'd done with his day; what he'd thought about; the art week at Bruford and how he needed an idea for a painting. An idea that was perfect.

But, of course, he didn't. Why would his dad be interested? In his dad's eyes, Clyde knew he wasn't the artist. That was Ashley.

To his dad, Clyde felt somehow … invisible.

He headed for the park. He wondered about texting Rick, but decided against it. If the other two Dixons were down there, fine. If not, he could people-watch. That was how Lizzi got ideas. Maybe it would work for him, too.

He crossed the road and wandered in through the park gates. There was no sign of Rick or Kevin. There weren't many people about at all.

A woman walked past pushing a pushchair with a toddler tucked into it fast asleep.

A man sat on a bench, reading a magazine. Another sat further away on the grass, eating chips from a bundle of paper with a little wooden fork.

Clyde stared at them. They must have stories. Everyone had stories. But nothing sprang into his head. No questions; no possibilities. Perhaps, like his bedroom, this was the wrong place to be; the wrong time of day to people-watch in the park.

He turned away to head back the way he'd come, when he heard a shout. He swung back. In the distance some boys played football. He hadn't spotted them before. They must have been hidden by the trees.

He wished he hadn't spotted them now.

They were Topz boys. And all of a sudden the four of them seemed to be looking in his direction.

Paul yelled and began to charge towards him.

'Dave! Dave-the-Rave!'

Clyde frowned; turned.

Dave-the-Rave stood a short way behind him. 'All right, Clyde?' he said.

Clyde stared at him. He couldn't make out why the Topz boy had spoken to him. Then he dropped his gaze.

'All right, Dave?' he grunted.

Paul reached them, breathing hard from his charge across the park. He gave Clyde a sideways glance, but ignored him.

'You came!' he puffed to Dave. 'Didn't think you were going to. You just missed a seriously impressive goal! Not mine obviously – I don't do seriously impressive goals. But we should get over there before you miss another one!'

He grabbed Dave's sleeve and went to pull him away. He didn't want to give Clyde the chance to be nasty. Not when his friend was back in the park for the first time since the last run-in with Dixons.

'Cool,' answered Dave. He didn't move. 'I'll be there in a minute.'

'But we should go *now*!' said Paul. Once more, his eyes flicked anxiously towards Clyde who stood, hands rammed into the pockets of his jeans, a scowl on his face.

'I'll be there in a minute,' Dave said again. 'It's OK.'

Paul still looked anxious, but he nodded; wandered slowly back to rejoin the game of football, snatching a few glances behind him as he went.

Dave faced Clyde awkwardly.

'I just wanted to say,' he mumbled, 'that I'm sorry for what I said in The Art Shop last week. I was in a bad mood.'

Clyde didn't speak. He didn't look at Dave. He just glared sullenly at the ground.

Dave stood for another moment, then began to walk away after Paul.

'Have you *always* believed in God?'

Dave stopped dead; turned his head to look at Clyde. 'Sorry?'

Clyde asked the question again. 'Have you always believed in God?'

Dave stared at the Dixons boy. Was this real? A *real* question, something he actually wanted to know? Or was it just another Dixons wind-up?

'Erm … yes,' he answered. 'Yes, I think I have.'

'And do you really think He cares about you? God? Do you really think you matter to Him?'

Dave was still suspicious. 'Yeah, I do,' he replied cautiously. 'One day I gave my life to Him and as soon as I did that, it meant I belonged to Him. He's promised to love me forever. It says so in the Bible … And I believe Him.'

Clyde gave a slight nod of his head, then returned his brooding gaze to the ground.

Eleven

Down towards the shopping centre, there was no sign of Lizzi. The walkway was busy with people. Clyde looked all around but she wasn't there.

He ran on towards the bakery. Perhaps she'd packed up for the day not long ago and he might find her on the bench there with a large take-away coffee.

Clyde slowed. There was a girl on the bench but it wasn't Lizzi. He was disappointed. He had something he wanted to tell her but he didn't know where she lived and she didn't have a mobile. She didn't like them.

'I just don't feel the need to be in touch with everyone the whole of the time,' she'd told him. 'If you have a mobile it's as if you can pre-arrange your entire life. I like bumping into people I'm not expecting to see; going places I didn't plan to go to. I like surprises.'

Which was all very well, Clyde thought, unless you wanted to speak to someone about a particular thing at a particular moment. Like he did right now. Then it was frustrating.

He was about to head home when he spotted her. Lizzi walked towards him, weighed down as usual by her holdall. She didn't notice him until he waved and called.

'Have you been drawing?' Clyde asked, nodding towards the holdall. 'You weren't on the walkway.'

'Got a new spot,' Lizzi smiled. 'Outside The Art Shop. The people who run it are friends of Mr Keller's. They said I could set up outside if I wanted to. So I did, and it's a great place to be. Guess what, Clyde?' she beamed. 'I've been doing portraits!'

Clyde grinned back at her. 'Then maybe we've both of us got more confidence today,' he said. 'Because I've worked out what my picture's going to be for the art week.'

'Fantastic!' Lizzi dropped the holdall to the ground. 'That thing weighs a ton!' she groaned. 'You're going to have a go at getting a place then? I knew you would!'

'I did what you said,' Clyde nodded. 'I went people-watching. In the park. First of all I looked around and I thought there was nobody there who could give me an idea about anything. But then I saw someone. Someone I don't even really like. And it was weird but – all of a sudden I knew what I wanted to paint.'

'Hah!' Lizzi laughed again. 'Those are always my best pictures. The ones that take me by surprise.'

'Do you want me to tell you about it?'

'No!' Lizzi brought a finger to her lips. 'Don't tell anyone – just paint it!'

Clyde hesitated. 'I wanted to ask you. It's just, I've pretty much run out of paint. And I haven't got any decent paper. And as soon as I've got some money I'll buy you more but I wondered if, until then …' His voice trailed off.

Lizzi didn't wait for him to finish. 'You can have whatever you need, Clyde.'

'I will give it you back,' he said quickly.

'You don't have to,' she answered, as if it was nothing at all. 'In fact, you could come back with me now and we could set you up. It's not far on the bus. I'm lucky. I have loads of stuff.'

'So how long have I got?' Clyde asked.

'What for?'

'To get my picture in.'

Lizzi shook her head. 'Sorry, can't remember. But it's on the flier.'

'OK,' said Clyde. 'Have you got one?'

'Not on me, but I dropped one round to your house earlier. You were out. I gave it to Ashley.'

Clyde looked puzzled. 'When?'

'Not sure. Around lunchtime, I suppose. I'd been drawing all morning and I was getting locked up sitting down all the time. I actually ran all the way. Are you impressed? You're right, your house is easy to find. Just as well, 'cos normally I can't find anywhere! It's going to be hilarious when I'm in Paris ...'

Clyde had stopped listening.

'But I was there at lunchtime,' he interrupted.

Lizzi broke off. 'Sorry?'

Clyde looked at her but didn't really see her. 'Did Ashley tell you I was out?'

'Well, yeah, but ... maybe she thought you *were*.'

Clyde spun round; started to stalk away.

'Clyde, wait!' Lizzi called. 'I thought you were coming back with me!'

He didn't turn; didn't answer.

'Honestly, Clyde, I'll bet she just didn't realise you were home!'

Clyde barely heard her. He was running now. Furious.

He cut through the alleyway behind Makepiece Avenue, running faster. He wanted Ashley to be home when he got there.

Suddenly, Rick and Kevin were in front of him. He jerked to a halt.

'What have you done with your phone?' Rick demanded. 'I've been texting.'

Clyde shook his head. He was out of breath.

'Didn't bring it.'

Rick frowned. 'What's up? You look like you're running away from someone.'

Again, Clyde shook his head.

'So where have you been?' asked Kevin.

'Nowhere,' snapped Clyde. 'It doesn't matter.'

'Glad you're in such a good mood,' said Kevin.

Clyde glared at him. 'What's it to you?'

'Mum's given me money for chips,' Kevin grunted. 'We thought you might wanna come. But, you know what, Clyde, just forget it!'

'Yeah,' Rick sniggered. 'All the more for us.'

They walked on. Clyde stood still; watched them.

'Look, I'm sorry, all right?' he called after them. 'I've just got to get home.'

'Yeah, right,' Rick muttered over his shoulder. He stopped briefly; turned to face the third Dixons boy. 'You know what your trouble is these days, don't you, Clyde?' he sneered. 'You spend *way* too much time hanging around with stuck-up arty girls.'

Clyde said nothing. He just stared. Rick's mouth twisted into a sideways smile, then he sauntered off with Kevin.

Outside the back door, Clyde paused a moment to kick off his trainers on the step. There was no one in the kitchen. He could see through the window.

He pushed down on the door handle and let himself in. He could hear the television blaring in the lounge. His dad was probably in there, feet up, with a cup of tea. He knew his mum would still be out. She had late shifts at work this week.

But where was Ashley?

Clyde stepped into the hall. The lounge door was

half open. He could see his dad on the sofa but he seemed to be on his own. Ashley always sat in the armchair under the window. It was empty. If Ashley was at home, she had to be in her room.

Clyde didn't speak to his dad. He went straight upstairs.

And he didn't knock on Ashley's door. He just shoved it open.

'Why did you tell Lizzi I was out?'

Ashley sat with her back to him in front of her laptop. She was watching something. She paused it and twisted round in her seat.

'Don't come in here without knocking,' was all she said.

'Why not?' Clyde snapped back. 'You do it to me all the time.'

Ashley looked at him disinterestedly. 'What do you want?'

'You *know*. Why did you tell Lizzi I was out earlier?'

'Did I?' Ashley shrugged. 'I don't think she wanted to see you.'

'She did!' growled Clyde. 'Why d'you think she came round? She asked for me, didn't she?'

'Don't remember.'

Clyde clenched his teeth together. 'Where's the flier she left?'

'What flier?'

'The flier she left for me! You know what I'm talking about, Ashley! What did you do with it?'

'Clyde, honestly,' said Ashley, 'I don't remember any flier. And if Lizzi left one, I don't *know* what I did with it. Now will you just go away, I was in the middle of watching something.'

She swung back in her seat.

Instantly, Clyde was beside her.

'You can't stop me going in for the art week,' he hissed. 'I know all about it anyway. Lizzi's already told me.'

'Bully for you,' said Ashley.

'We're friends now, her and me! She's gonna help me! I know Dad thinks you're the *only* artist in the family, but d'you know what, I don't care!' Clyde's voice was rising; getting louder and louder. 'I don't care what *he* thinks and I don't care what *you* think! You know nothing! *Nothing*! But Lizzi does – and Lizzi believes in me. She *believes* in me!'

'What's going on?'

Their dad's voice barked up the stairs.

'Clyde? I didn't even know you were home.'

Rob stood in the bedroom doorway. 'Well?' he demanded. 'Am I really going to have to ask you again?'

Ashley stood up; shook her head. 'It's nothing, Dad. Clyde was just getting a bit confused, that's all.'

'I'm not confused!' Clyde retorted.

Ashley ignored him. 'He's been hanging around that girl, Lizzi. She's the one from school who's been doing the pavement art. She called round earlier and I told her Clyde was out. It seemed like the best thing to do.'

'What do you mean "the best thing to do"?' Clyde shouted. 'Best for who?'

'Best for *you*, Clyde.' Ashley hesitated. 'It's a bit awkward really. She came round to tell you to leave her alone. She said she didn't want kids trailing after her. I thought you'd be upset, Clyde, so that's why I told her you weren't here.'

Clyde's jaw dropped. Ashley could twist anything – *anything* – around to make a totally believable lie!

'That's not true,' he muttered. 'I've just seen her, I know that's not true!'

'Everyone gets crushes now and then, Clyde,' said Ashley. 'It's nothing to be ashamed of.'

'Oh, is that what it is!' grinned Rob. 'A crush! For a minute I thought it was something serious. Never mind, Clyde. You'll get over it.'

Clyde stepped towards him; clenched his fists furiously.

'I haven't got a crush,' he said. There was a tremble in his voice. 'Lizzi's my friend. A real friend. A *proper* friend. She wants to help me. That's why she came round here. To give me a flier about an art week. She thinks I should try to get on it, Dad, because Ashley's not the only one who's good at art in this house!'

He paused. Swallowed.

'*I'm* good at art, too, Dad. Lizzi's told me I am. So I think that's what I want to do: get better and better, and *be* an artist. And I know you'll never believe it because nothing I do matters to you, but d'you know what? I don't care. For the first time ever, I *really* don't care! 'Cos I'm just going to do it anyway!'

He shoved his way out of the bedroom and tore down the stairs. He heard his dad's shouts: 'Clyde, what's the matter now? Can't you take a joke? Clyde, come back here!'

He took no notice; just slammed the back door on his way out.

Twelve

R U awake?

Dave punched in the text and sent it to Paul. He held on to his phone as he lay in bed, and waited. Almost instantly it bleeped.

Might be, Paul texted back.

Dave jabbed in another message: *Can't sleep. SO weird wot happened in park with Clyde.*

Yeah. MEGA weird, was Paul's reply.

Dave texted: *Wot shud I do? Talk 2 him again?*

Paul answered: *Pray I reckon. Greg wud say pray.*

Will U pray 2?

Course.

Dave dropped the phone onto his bedside table. He rolled over and pulled his duvet up to his ears.

Five minutes later, the phone was back in his hand and he'd sent another text.

R U still awake?

Think so, Paul texted back.

Dave's thumb hit at the keys: *I felt like a lamp 2day. Like God says we shud be.*

Cool. Told U not 2 hide.

Yeah. Thanks.

No probs.

R U sleepy? Dave asked.

Not really. U?

Dave answered: *Nah.*

Has ur thumb got cramp yet? Paul replied.

Yeah.

Night then, texted Paul.

Night, answered Dave.

Once more Dave put the phone down and lay on his back in the half-light staring up at the ceiling. The orange glow from the street lamps along the road outside seeped in around the edges of his curtains.

Dave propped himself up on his elbows. It was a warm night. Too warm to be in bed with the window closed. He heaved himself upright, pulled back one curtain and pushed the window open. Immediately, he could hear the sounds of Holly Hill. Cars trundled about. On the street below, someone was talking. Dave could only make out one man's voice, so he thought he must be on the phone. Further away, a siren wailed. And for as far as he could see, the street lamps shone their orange light, chasing away the darkness.

Overhead the sky was peppered with stars and the moon hung in the middle of them like a huge lantern.

Your world is full of light, isn't it, God? It was the first thing You made when You created the universe. 'Let there be light,' You said, and there was.

Dave didn't move from the window as he prayed. It helped him to look up into the sky; to imagine God setting the moon and the stars in their places. It made him feel that God was very close.

*I'm sorry about before; about wanting to hide my light away. I think sometimes I feel like Dixons don't deserve to know You. They don't deserve Your love. They're so mean I'm not sure they deserve to be loved by anybody. I reckon all of us in Topz feel like that sometimes. So I'm sorry for that, too, because You want **everyone** to get to know You. And the only way that can happen is if people like me, people like Topz – people all over the world who know and love You – tell all the people who don't. That man down there right now talking on his phone. I wonder if **he** knows You. I wonder if anyone's ever told him about You.*

Why is talking about You so hard, God? It shouldn't be, should it? When I'm excited about something on TV, I tell everyone! 'You've got to watch it!' I go on and on! When I'm excited about anything really, I can't keep it to myself.

Being Your friend should be like that – SO exciting that we just can't keep quiet about it. We should all be like – 'You can be friends with God, too! Forever and ever! The Creator of the whole universe, the One who made light out of nothing – He loves you and He wants to be Your Friend NOW! Right this second! What are you waiting for? Give your life to Him! It's the most awesome thing ever!'

But I don't know what it is, God. I suppose we get scared that people will laugh at us and think we're stupid. Or scared that they'll make fun of us and pick on us. Because that's what Dixons do, isn't it, and that's why they do it. They pick on us because of You.

*I told You I wanted to be like Jesus, didn't I, God? I don't want it to matter how I feel. I don't want it to make a difference whether I'm scared or not. I **still** want to tell people about You because they need to know. I want to be the light You want me to be.*

*Clyde asked me questions today. He's never done that before. And if I hadn't been in the park just at that minute, he might **not** have asked them. Not ever. Please, God, please put me in the right place to talk to him again. If he asks questions or not, please make me brave.*

I keep thinking, God, that if one of the Dixons Gang gives his life to You then, who knows? The other two just might, too.

Beside his bed, Dave's phone bleeped. He reached for it. Paul had texted.
R U still awake?
   He texted back: *Might be.*
   Paul texted: *Night again then.*
   Dave grinned and punched in a final message: *Night again.*

Clyde stared through his bedroom window. The sun streamed in. It would be another warm day. He watched his dad walk down the front path and turn left along the pavement on his way to work at the supermarket. He kept watching until he'd disappeared.

Glancing round, he checked the time. Ten o'clock. He guessed his dad wouldn't be back till after six that evening.

He stood up, stretched and yawned. He'd stayed out at the park late the night before. He hadn't wanted to go home. All Ashley seemed to do was lie and all his dad did was shout. Why would he want to go back to that?

His mum had texted; asked him to come home; told him supper was ready. He'd replied that he wasn't hungry. He'd be back later.

Much later as it turned out.

But Clyde was hungry now. He'd waited to have breakfast until his dad had gone out. He went to his bedroom door; opened it quietly. Then he slipped downstairs to the kitchen.

'I was just about to come up and see you,' said his mum. 'I didn't know if you were awake.'

Clyde helped himself to cereal; poured on the milk. He glanced at her. She didn't ask what had happened yesterday. But the question was there in her eyes.

'It wasn't my fault,' Clyde muttered. 'Ashley's a liar.'

His mum gazed at him. She looked sad. Tired. So often that's how she looked.

'What are you up to today?' she asked.

'Nothing,' Clyde grunted. He made for the kitchen door,

then turned to add, 'Well, nothing that matters.'

Back in his room, Clyde wolfed down his breakfast.

It wasn't true what he'd said to his mum. What he wanted to do today *did* matter. To him it mattered enormously. He just didn't think it would matter to anyone else.

He pulled open his desk drawers and rifled through them. He needed paper – good-sized paper. He'd be able to get some from Lizzi when he saw her again; paints, too. But he didn't know when that would be and he wanted to make a start on his picture. He could plan it out today. If he made a rough sketch he'd be able to transfer it to the proper paper when he had it.

He found one half-finished exercise book. It was too small, but it seemed to be the only paper he had left. Even a double page wasn't big enough. Still, it would have to do.

Clyde had an image for his picture in his head. It had begun to form itself when his dad had arrived home from work the day before.

It somehow became clear a little later when he'd seen Topz in the park.

Lizzi had told him that his question mark tree wasn't a sad picture. To her that wasn't the way it felt. What would she make of his new idea, he wondered? She probably wouldn't understand it. Clyde wasn't sure whether anyone would. But perhaps that didn't matter. As Lizzi had said, everyone who looked at it would make sense of it in their own way.

He grasped a pencil and drew. Very slowly, the picture started to take shape. Just as with the tree, Clyde began sections, rubbed them out, started again. This sketch was only supposed to be rough, but he knew that if he could get it right – if he could just capture what he felt *exactly* – then he'd have more confidence when it came to creating the real thing.

He kept working away. He was thirsty but he didn't stop for a drink. It was only when his mum called up the stairs that lunch was ready that he realised the time. He dropped his pencil onto his desk and rubbed his eyes. He was almost finished. The picture still wasn't quite perfect but that didn't matter so much now. He liked what he'd done. It *felt* how he wanted it to feel.

The perfect picture must be the one he'd give in to the art teachers at Bruford.

Clyde's mum called again. He went downstairs to the kitchen and sat at the table with Ashley. The two of them munched sandwiches in silence. Cathy appeared in the doorway dressed ready for work.

'Right, I'm off,' she said. 'I should be back about eight.' She hesitated. 'Please, you two, no more fighting, eh?'

Ashley shook her head. 'Too busy revising for my exams. Haven't got time to fight.'

'Hooray for exams then,' Cathy replied.

She turned to go when her mobile rang in her bag.

'Oh, who's this?' she mumbled. 'I'm going to be late.' She waved at Clyde and Ashley and headed for the front door. 'Hello, Pete. What are you doing ringing me? Rob's in today. Haven't you seen him?'

Clyde heard his mum gasp. He twisted his head to look through the doorway into the hall. He saw her turn to him as her face went white.

'I'm supposed to be at work,' she murmured. 'I'll have to phone.'

'What is it?' Clyde asked. 'What's happened?'

Cathy stood in the kitchen doorway, pale and trembling.

'It's your dad,' she said. 'There's been some sort of accident. He was in the warehouse and a load of shelving fell over on top of him. He's unconscious, Pete says. The ambulance is there. They're taking him to hospital.'

Ashley stared at her. 'Is he all right?'

Clyde's mum shook her head. 'I don't know. I really don't know. We need to get over there. Clyde, go and get your shoes on.'

Clyde stood up; lurched towards the front door. He put a hand out to steady himself as he thrust his feet into his trainers. He was cold.

It was hot outside but he was **freezing cold**.

Thirteen

To Clyde, the hospital felt strange. Noisy but oddly silent at the same time. Nurses marched purposefully to and fro. They checked equipment, adjusted tubes and made notes on clipboards. They stood in corners and exchanged the odd quiet word. Trolleys trundled past, phones rang, monitors beeped and lights flashed.

But no one could give them any news. As far as finding out how his dad was – how badly he'd been hurt – there was silence. No one seemed able to tell them anything. He was still unconscious. That's all they knew.

After what seemed like ages, a doctor did come to speak to them. She said they were doing everything possible. Rob's right arm and leg had been broken in the accident and he was badly bruised, but it was the injury to his head that worried them the most.

Clyde's mum was in tears. 'Will he be all right, though?' she sobbed. 'Can you at least tell me that? Will he be all right?'

'This is very early stages still, Mrs Bicton,' the doctor said. 'Let's just wait and see how things develop.'

They were taken through to see him. He lay in a bed at the far end of the ward. There were pale blue curtains drawn almost the whole way around. His dad looked comfortable, Clyde thought. He could just be sleeping.

Except that he was surrounded by tubes and wires, and a machine beside the bed bleeped repetitively. He wasn't asleep. He was badly hurt.

There was one chair by the bed and a nurse pulled up a couple more for them.

'Can I get you anything?' he asked. 'A cup of tea?'

Cathy smiled. 'A cup of tea would be lovely, thank you,' she gulped. 'Tea for you, Ashley?'

Ashley nodded.

The nurse looked at Clyde. 'And what about you, young man?'

Clyde shook his head. 'Nothing, thanks.'

'Are you sure?' the nurse said kindly. 'How about a hot chocolate? You need to keep your strength up.'

Again, Clyde shook his head. He sat down; leaned forward, peered into his dad's face. It felt weird to see him lying so completely still. Clyde and his dad didn't talk to each other much. When they did, his dad was often stern and Clyde was snappy. In Clyde's mind, his dad's face always frowned, always seemed cross.

But looking at him now, bruised and battered and pale, he didn't look cross at all. Oddly, Clyde thought, it was almost like looking at a stranger.

Cathy and Ashley drank their tea. The nurse hovered, checked the monitors, adjusted the tubes, made notes on the clipboard. The doctor came back and the nurse told her there had been no change. She nodded, smiled at Cathy, then disappeared again.

Clyde's eyes felt suddenly sore. He'd been staring at his dad for so long he wondered if he'd forgotten to blink. He rubbed at them with the back of his hands.

'Are you all right, love?' His mum touched his shoulder.

'What time is it?' he asked.

She glanced at her watch. 'Half past four.'

Clyde chewed at his thumbnail. 'Can I go outside for a bit?' he asked.

'Oh, I'm not sure that's a good idea, Clyde,' murmured his mum. 'I don't want you to get lost. There are so many corridors in this place. Maybe Ashley should go with you.'

'I won't get lost,' Clyde answered quickly. 'There are signs all over the place. I just want to be on my own, I want to go for a walk. I'll be back in a bit.'

He slipped through the blue curtains.

'Have you got your phone?' his mum called softly.

'Yeah.' Clyde made his way to the end of the ward.

The nurse looking after his dad sat behind a desk in the corridor outside. He was on the phone. As Clyde walked past he glanced up and waved. Clyde gave him a nod in return.

He didn't take the lift. He found the staircase, hung onto the banister and ran down the stairs as fast as he could. He'd been sitting still for so long, he just wanted to move; didn't want to stop. He hurried outside through the main entrance doors, turned right and began to hurtle along the pavement. The air was still warm but it was cooler than inside the hospital. It was fresher, too. Clyde breathed it in deeply.

He wasn't sure where to go, but did it really matter? All he wanted to do was to run. The hospital wasn't far from the shopping centre. Perhaps he could run all the way there and all the way back. If he ran hard and fast, he'd stop thinking, wouldn't he? He'd have to focus on his pace, his breathing. Then maybe he could get that picture out of his head: his dad, lying in bed. Hurt and white and still.

Up ahead a small crowd of people stood together at a bus stop. They blocked the pavement. Clyde needed to step out into the road to get around them, but as he drew closer, he realised he couldn't because a bus was about to pull in. He slowed. Stopped for a moment. As soon as there was a gap on the pavement, he'd push on through.

He leant forward, hands on his knees, trying to get his breath back. He was only vaguely aware of a knocking sound. It was when he thought he heard someone call his name that he glanced up.

Lizzi was on the bus. She banged on the window to try to get his attention. She waved and laughed.

Then she saw the look on his face.

Her smile froze. 'What's wrong?' she mouthed.

Clyde continued to gaze at her through the window. In an instant she was on her feet. There were people still trying to get onto the bus, but she barged down the aisle, shoving her holdall in front of her, murmuring, 'Sorry, sorry, I've got to get off.'

Outside on the pavement, she set the holdall on the ground and peered at Clyde intently.

'What's wrong?' she asked. 'What's happened?'

Clyde blinked at her. He didn't seem to have heard her. 'Why are you here?' he murmured. 'Do you know about my dad?'

'I've been doing portraits all day. I was on my way home. I don't know anything about anything, so just tell me, Clyde, please. What's happened?'

They sat together on the pavement under the bus shelter. Lizzi listened; watched Clyde's face as he talked.

'I'm so sorry, Clyde,' she said quietly. 'What can I do to help? Just tell me and I'll do it.'

Clyde shook his head. 'There's nothing. We have to wait. The doctor says we've just got to wait.'

He fell silent and began to chew his thumbnail again.

Lizzi prodded him gently. 'Don't do that, you'll make it sore.'

Clyde dropped his hand into his lap. 'I'm not close to Dad,' he mumbled. 'A lot of the time it's like we're not really *anything* to each other. Like we don't even know each other.'

His eyes flicked towards Lizzi. 'I know you don't know your dad or your mum. But I see my dad every day. We live together in the same house, and I don't know why but he doesn't seem to notice me. Not properly. Some days I don't even think he looks at me. Or when he does look he doesn't see me.'

Clyde screwed up his face; swallowed hard. 'And now this has happened ...' He shrugged. 'I mean what if he never has the chance to see me? Not ever? What if he never opens his eyes, Lizzi?'

'Of *course* he will!' Lizzi reached out and squeezed his arm. 'You've got to believe that, Clyde! It's only just happened, hasn't it? Just a few hours ago? His body's probably just saying, "Hey! Leave me alone for five minutes, I've had a bang on the head!" He *will* open his eyes, Clyde. And he *will* see you.'

Several people now stood near them at the edge of the shelter, waiting for the next bus.

'You should go,' Clyde said.

Lizzi shook her head. 'I'm not in any hurry.'

They sat in silence until Clyde muttered, 'I ought to get back in there.'

'OK.'

Then, 'I did a rough sketch of my picture,' Clyde said. 'I'd just finished it when this happened.'

Lizzi's eyes widened. 'That reminds me!' She turned to the holdall, unzipped it and fished about inside. 'I brought you some stuff. Paper and paints – just what you asked for. I thought I'd bring it with me in case I saw you down at the shopping centre. I didn't know if you might come looking for me.' She paused. 'Never thought I'd see you up here.'

She handed Clyde a carrier bag. 'If there's anything else you need, you just let me know.'

Clyde nodded. 'Thanks,' he murmured.

'Anything else at all,' Lizzi repeated. 'Promise me you'll ask.'

'I promise.'

A bus rolled in. The waiting passengers climbed on board. Lizzi hoicked her holdall in behind them; found a seat. She waved as they pulled out into the traffic.

Clyde, his face tired and pinched, waved one hand back. The carrier bag was clasped tightly in the other.

Fourteen

The news of Rob Bicton's accident seemed to spread quickly around Holly Hill. A string of text messages bleeped into Cathy, Clyde and Ashley's phones. Rick sent several and signed them from Kevin, too, since Kevin didn't have a mobile. When they got home late that night, friends had left messages of love and concern and offers of help on the house phone, too.

There was nothing to tell anyone. No news.

Rob still hadn't woken up.

Clyde didn't go to bed. He didn't want to. If he closed his eyes, he wouldn't sleep. Inside his head he'd still see his dad lying in hospital.

Instead, he sat at his desk. He laid the pad of paper Lizzi had given him open in front of him in the pool of light from his lamp. With the rough sketch he'd drawn earlier there to guide him, he began to work on his picture. He drew and rubbed out; drew once more. He changed things; changed them back. Twice he even started all over again. Just as with The Story Tree, the picture was so clear in his mind. He wanted the image he put onto the paper to match it exactly in every detail.

Finally, when enough outlines were in place, Clyde began to paint. He painted on through what was left of the night. He never lifted his eyes from the picture, not once, until it was finished.

When at last he put the paintbrush down and leaned back in his chair to stretch out his arms, he realised it was getting light.

He stood up. He felt stiff and cold from having

stayed awake all night. He stretched again, yawned. Then he dropped back onto his chair; gazed down at the painting.

It was mostly of clouds. They were grey and thick with soft outlines. They overlapped, one on top of the other. In patches, the grey was darker, more shadowy. At the edges of the cloud mass, Clyde had brushed pale yellow, as if there was a bright light somewhere in behind. But the clouds were so dense that only a thin glow escaped around them.

And in just a few places, hardly there at all, were the tiniest glimpses of two pillars. They stood, one on each side of the picture, almost completely swathed in the cloudbank.

Clyde didn't know if the painting was good; good enough to get him a place on the art week. He didn't know if anyone would like or even understand it. But just at that moment, he didn't care. It made perfect sense to *him* and that's all that mattered.

There was a knock on his door. He jumped up to open it.

His mum stood there. 'Clyde, you don't look as if you've been to bed.'

'I haven't,' he said.

She sighed. 'I'm going back to the hospital soon. Do you want to come?'

Clyde nodded.

'I'll sort us all out a bit of breakfast, then,' she said.

An hour later the three of them were ready to go. No one from the hospital had rung. At least that must mean Rob hadn't got any worse overnight. Clyde guessed it also meant that he hadn't got any better.

He dashed back up to his bedroom.

The painting still lay on his desk. He leaned over it. It looked just about dry, apart from a couple of very small patches.

He pulled open a drawer and picked out a black felt tip pen. As neatly as he could, in one corner at the bottom of the paper, he wrote the picture's title. Then he laid another sheet of paper carefully over the painting, closed the sketchpad and slipped it into his rucksack.

He sat in the back seat of the car behind Ashley as his mum drove them to the hospital. He hoped there would be a few moments in the day when he could be with his dad by himself. There were things he wanted to say; things he wanted to tell him. Clyde knew his dad probably wouldn't be able to hear him. Not if he still hadn't woken up.

But somehow he felt it would be easier to talk to him now that he'd painted his picture. He'd be able to explain to his dad how he felt because he could talk about what the painting meant.

And Clyde could tell him why he'd called it *The Cloudgate Mystery*.

The beeps from the machine by Rob's bed throbbed into Cathy Bicton's head.

The three of them had talked as much as they could; to each other; to Rob. But the conversation had run dry and now they sat in silence.

At about one o'clock, Clyde's mum said what Clyde had hoped she would: 'I think we may as well pop home for some lunch. We can come back later. They'll ring if there's any news.'

'I'll stay here,' Clyde said. 'I'm not really hungry.'

'Come on, love,' said his mum. 'We could all do with a break.'

'I'm fine,' Clyde answered. 'I'll stay till you get back.'

Just after Cathy and Ashley had left, the nurse from the day before came in to make his checks.

'Hello there,' he said. 'Keeping your dad company again, I see.'

'Is he getting better?' Clyde asked.

'Well,' smiled the nurse, 'he's not getting any worse, that's the main thing at the moment. But what we really want him to do is wake up. You have a chat with him. I'll be back in a while.' He gave Clyde a wink and pulled the blue curtain closed behind him as he left.

Clyde sat still. He listened to the beeps of the machine. He watched his dad's chest rise and fall as he breathed in and out.

He began to talk.

'Time to wake up, Dad. You always tell me off when *I* have long lie-ins. This must be the longest lie-in ever.'

He paused; leaned back in his chair and listened through the curtains. There were the usual sounds from the ward, but they were distant. No one was about to disturb them.

He bent down, unzipped his rucksack and pulled out the sketchpad.

'I've got something to show you, Dad. I hope it's not gonna make you cross. I know you think Ashley's the artist in our family, and maybe she is. Maybe I'm not an artist – maybe I never will be – but the thing is, I really love art. I didn't used to. I used to think it was stupid like I thought everything at school was stupid. But I think that changed when I found out I could do it. I could draw. I could see things in my head and put them down on paper.

'The last time we saw each other before … before this happened … we had a sort of fight. Do you remember?

I don't really know what you're going to remember when you wake up. But it was Ashley who started it, winding me up like she does. I know you won't want to believe it, but she tells lies, Dad. She's always trying to make me look bad.'

Clyde listened to the beep of the machine; watched his dad's breathing.

'Anyway, that doesn't matter now. Like I said, I've got something to show you.'

He flipped the sketchpad open to his painting; gazed down at it as he talked.

'I painted a picture. It's called *The Cloudgate Mystery*. Stupid title, but I quite like it. There's a gateway – a big wide gateway, with pillars on either side. But you can't see much because of the clouds. They're thick, really thick, and they're dark in places. So you can't see much of the pillars, or the gateway, or what's through it on the other side.

'There must be something good through it, though, because there's light there somewhere. You can see it round the edges of the clouds.

'But it's not just being on *this* side of the clouds that means you can't see. Whatever's *behind* the clouds and *through* the gateway can't see out either.

'Here.' Clyde lifted the painting; held it up in front of his Dad's face.

'There's an art week at Bruford in the summer holidays. If you paint something they like, you get a place. And I really want a place, I *really* do. And this is the picture that came into my head to paint.'

He lowered the pad back down onto his lap. Stared at his dad intently.

'You see, Dad, this picture is how I feel about me.

'I feel like it when I'm anywhere near that Topz Gang.

They talk about God like He's their Friend. Like He *knows* them. He's *interested* in them. Like *He* can see them and *they* can see Him.

'And I hate them because it's not like that for me. God can't see *me*. He's not even looking. Why would He want to? What am I worth to God? Nothing … I'm not even worth anything to you, and you're my dad.

'So I painted the gateway to heaven and I covered it in clouds because I can't see in and God can't see out. And I called it *The Cloudgate Mystery* because that's what it is – a mystery and I don't understand it. The Topz Gang reckon God loves everyone … So why doesn't He love me?'

Clyde glanced down and closed the pad.

'And it's not just God who's lost somewhere in the clouds, Dad,' he murmured. 'It's you, too. That's another mystery. You're my dad but we don't seem to know each other. It's like we can't see each other. You're on one side of the gateway and I'm on the other. And there are all those clouds in between.'

Clyde sat silent for a moment. He searched his dad's face gazing at his closed eyes.

'Wake up, Dad,' he whispered. 'The last time I spoke to you, I was cross. I'm sorry. Please wake up. I want you to hear what I'm saying. I want you to open your eyes and see me.'

The hospital ward was warm. Clyde's eyelids felt heavy and he let them droop. He listened to the sounds on the other side of the blue curtains. The beeping machines, the trundle of trolleys, footsteps clacking on the hard floors, the murmur of voices. He listened until all the different sounds merged into one dull, constant noise … Until they faded into silence.

Fifteen

Clyde woke with a start. He opened his eyes. Everything around him seemed blurred and his head felt muzzy. For an instant, he didn't know where he was. He blinked hard; saw his dad lying in the hospital bed. At once it all flooded back.

Clyde wondered how long he'd been asleep. He lifted his arms to stretch.

That's when he remembered his painting.

He looked down. The sketchpad had been on his lap. He'd gone to sleep holding it. But now it wasn't there. He must have dropped it while he slept.

He leaned forward to look on the floor and under the bed.

'Are you after this?'

Startled, Clyde twisted round. Ashley stood just behind him. She held the sketchpad open in front of her and studied the Cloudgate picture.

Clyde stared at her. A glint of anger crept into his eyes. 'Give that back,' he growled.

'What, this funny little drawing?' Ashley answered. There was a sneer in her voice. 'Did *you* do it?'

Clyde jumped to his feet. 'Just give it back!'

'What's it meant to be, Clyde?'

'It's nothing to do with you. You'd never get it.' Clyde couldn't shout. Not in here. He didn't even have the energy. He just wanted the picture back.

'Where's Mum?' he whispered.

'Talking to the doctor,' Ashley said.

Clyde held out a hand. 'Seriously, Ashley, give it back to me now. It's not yours. You shouldn't even be looking at it.'

Ashley carried on as if he hadn't spoken. 'Who's it for, Clyde? Is it for Dad? Did you bring it here so you could show him if he happens to wake up?' She shook her head. '*If* Dad wakes up, Clyde, he's not going to care about your stupid drawings. They're not important. *You're* not important. And this?' She held up the picture. 'I'm sorry, to burst your pathetic, pointless artistic bubble but – it's trash.'

Clyde lunged for the pad but Ashley snatched it away.

'You never leave me alone!' Clyde hissed. 'Why don't you *ever* leave me alone?'

He made another grab for it. This time his hands closed around it and he yanked hard. Ashley gazed at him. A scornful stare right into his eyes.

Suddenly she let go and Clyde jerked backwards. He almost lost his balance and fell into the bed.

'If I were you I'd give up now, Clyde, before you end up getting disappointed,' Ashley said quietly. 'You've got no chance of getting on that art week. I don't know what Lizzi's told you but they're going to want kids who've actually got talent. Mr Keller's tough, Clyde. Really tough. And he's not going to want someone like you who's got absolutely no talent at all.'

Behind Ashley, the blue curtains parted.

Clyde's mum stood in the opening. She made the effort to smile but there were tears in her eyes.

Ashley turned. 'What did they say?'

Cathy shook her head. 'No change,' she murmured. 'Imagine that. All those times he's gone on and on and on and I've just wanted him to be quiet.' She pressed her lips together, struggled not to cry. 'Now I'd do anything for him to be wide-awake and ranting. But it's not going to happen, is it? It's not going to happen.'

Clyde saw in a moment that his mum had all but given up hope.

'It will, though, won't it?' he said. 'It will. Mum?'

His mum looked empty somehow. Almost hollow. There were dark circles under her eyes. She barely looked at him. And there was nothing he could do and nothing he could say.

All of a sudden, Clyde pushed his way through the curtains. His mum didn't try to stop him. He took the stairs and headed out through the main entrance. The sketchpad was still clasped tightly in his hands. He walked quickly. He wanted to get to the shopping centre before it was too late. Before Lizzi had packed up for the day and gone home.

It was busy out. There were people everywhere. He dodged them. Weaved between them. He didn't slow down until The Art Shop was in sight.

Lizzi was still there. A boy of about eight years old sat on a stool in front of her while she worked away at her easel. A woman stood close by and watched and smiled. Probably the boy's mum.

Clyde watched, too, from a distance. He waited until the boy's caricature was finished and the boy and his mum had giggled at it, cooed over it, and wandered away.

'Why did you have to tell me about that art week?'

Lizzi turned to find Clyde standing behind her. Her face broke into a wide smile. 'Clyde! How's your dad?'

'It doesn't matter,' Clyde answered. 'Why did you have to tell me about the art week, Lizzi?'

Lizzi frowned. 'I thought you might enjoy it, Clyde.'

Clyde looked at her; shook his head. 'D'you know what I wish?' he gulped. 'I wish I'd never met you!'

Lizzi gazed back at him, distraught. 'What? Why? What have I done?'

'You believed in me!' Clyde cried wretchedly. 'You believed in me and you made *me* believe in me, too!'

'But that's a good thing! That's a good thing, isn't it, Clyde?'

'No!' he snarled. 'Because I'm not worth anything, Lizzi! And I've always known that but now it feels so much worse because just for a second – a *second* – I thought I was … I thought I *could* be.'

He looked down at the sketchpad in his hands; dropped it at her feet.

'You can have this back,' he muttered. 'I don't need it any more.'

The ball sailed over Dave's head. Benny's kick had launched it high and hard at Topz's makeshift goal.

'Yesss!' Benny yelled. 'You make this so easy, Dave-the-Rave!'

Dave scowled at him. The more goals Benny scored, the louder he crowed. He was beginning to wish Benny and Danny had turned up at the park with their bikes rather than a football.

He turned and ran to pick the ball up – for what felt like the hundredth time.

But this time he spotted the Dixons boy.

Clyde sat cross-legged on the grass by himself on the far side of the skateboard park. He slouched forward, his head in his hands. He didn't seem aware of the Topz Gang; didn't seem aware of anyone.

Dave grabbed the ball and ran back to Benny and Danny.

'Clyde's over there,' he said. 'I'm gonna go and talk to him.'

He wandered over to where the Dixon sat on the grass.

'Clyde?' he said.

Clyde raised his head slightly; flicked his eyes towards Dave. He said nothing.

'I know you probably don't care what I think – what any of Topz think,' Dave began again. 'But we're really sorry about your dad. It's awful.'

Still Clyde didn't speak.

'Are you … OK?' Stupid question, Dave thought, the moment it was out of his mouth.

Clyde glanced at him again. 'Do I look OK to you?'

'No.' Dave shook his head. 'No, I'm an idiot. Sorry.'

Clyde studied his thumbnail. There wasn't much of it left but he chewed at it anyway.

'Yeah, but you don't *really* think you're an idiot, do you, Dave?' he grunted. ''Cos you're all right, aren't you? All you Topz? Everything's so easy for you.'

Dave wasn't sure what he meant; didn't know how to answer.

Clyde stared at him hard now. 'Everyone believes in you, don't they, Topzy? Everyone thinks you're great! You're so *good*! Don't you get bored with that? With being good *all* the time? I bet you never did anything wrong in your whole life.'

Dave hesitated a moment. Then he sat down on the grass.

'I bet you I did,' he said. 'I do plenty of wrong things. The only difference between me and you is that when I *do* do something wrong, I tell God I'm sorry.'

'Oh, yeah,' sneered Clyde, 'because God's just such a good mate of yours, isn't He?'

'Yeah,' said Dave. 'Actually He is.'

Clyde almost laughed. A weird, strangled sound that seemed to catch in his throat.

'You know, you're wrong about the only difference between us,' he muttered. 'D'you wanna know what it *really* is? The *real* difference between you and me, Dave, is that – ' He broke off. A huge sob shook him. He swallowed it down. 'The real difference is that God can see you. He looks at you and He thinks, *Yeah, he's all right is that Dave. All of those Topz Gang, they're OK. They're worth something. I can love them because they're not useless and they're not a waste of space!*'

And then the tears came. 'But *me*? What am *I* worth, Dave? God can't see me and I can't see Him! He doesn't even know I exist and if He did He wouldn't care! So just tell me, Dave, just tell me, WHAT IS THE POINT OF ME?'

Clyde hid his face in his hands. He couldn't speak any more. His shoulders shuddered. All he could do was sit there on the grass and sob.

Dave stared at him. What had Clyde just said? *What is the point of me?*

That was the same question Dave had asked about Dixons only a few weeks before.

And he felt ashamed.

'*I* can't change how you feel,' Dave said quietly. 'But God can. 'Cos you're so wrong, Clyde. God *does* know you exist because He made you. He knew you before you were even born. He's got a plan for you, a purpose – a *point*. He knows what you're good at and what'll make you happy. And all He's waiting for, to show You how much He loves you, is for you to want to be His friend.'

Dave paused. Clyde still sobbed but more quietly.

'God sees you all the time, Clyde. Wherever you are; whatever you're doing. Right now even, He knows where you are. We can't hide from Him even if we want to because God doesn't keep His eyes closed. They're *always wide open*. So if you want to find Him, Clyde,' Dave added gently, 'if you decide you want to be His friend – then you're the one who needs to open yours.'

Sixteen

On Sunday morning, Clyde was up early.

It was almost a week since his dad's accident. He and his mum and Ashley had gone to the hospital every day. It felt as if they were living on a different planet. All around them life carried on as normal, but they were somehow separate from it; locked into their own world of sadness and anxiety and not knowing.

Then, on the Friday, late in the evening, when they'd been at the hospital for hours and were just about to go home, Clyde's dad had opened his eyes.

He looked at them.

He squeezed their hands.

He even smiled. He smiled when he looked at Clyde. A smile full of warmth and love and affection.

Clyde felt as though his dad had seen him for the very first time.

The following afternoon, Clyde had run from the hospital to the shopping centre. He'd headed straight for The Art Shop. There was no sign of Lizzi. No stool, no easel, no holdall. She wasn't drinking coffee on the bench outside the baker's either. Nor could he see her on the walkway, although there was a new picture there. People crowded round to look at it. It showed a large, rectangular window, divided into nine panes. Through the window was a view of hills and valleys, streams and waterfalls. And in the distance, perched on the top of the farthest hill, was a castle, with high turrets topped with flags dancing in an invisible breeze. It was magical.

Clyde peered through the clusters of people.

Where was she? Where *was* Lizzi? The picture looked fresh and new. Perhaps she hadn't long finished it.

He remembered her spotting him near the hospital through the bus window on her way home. If she'd only just left, she might still be on her way to the bus stop now.

The closest one was just round the corner. Clyde ran again. He stopped at the pelican crossing and pressed the button, waiting impatiently for the green man to appear. He hurtled across the road. Then he slowed and his shoulders sagged in disappointment.

There were two girls standing at the bus stop. Neither of them was Lizzi.

Clyde was hot and his throat was dry. He was so close to home now, he thought he might as well call in there for a drink before heading back to the hospital. He texted his mum to let her know. Then he made his way back to the Dixons Estate, cutting through the alleyway behind Makepiece Avenue.

As he emerged at the other end, he turned right.

He walked with his head down, so it was Lizzi who saw him first.

'That's weird,' she said. 'I've just been round your house looking for you.'

Clyde glanced up. 'Weirder still,' he replied, 'I've been round *everywhere* looking for *you*.'

'I heard your dad woke up,' Lizzi said. 'I'm really pleased, Clyde. For him and for you.'

Clyde nodded.

'So why were you looking for me?' Lizzi asked. 'You're not going to shout at me again, are you?'

'No,' Clyde said. ''Course not.'

Lizzi gave him a half smile. 'That's good. Although I

did draw myself a castle today. I thought if you started shouting again I could run away and hide in it.'

Clyde smiled back. 'I saw it. I saw the picture. It's brilliant. There were loads of people looking.'

'I know!' She looked pleased. 'When you live in a town I think you need some countryside to gaze at. Especially countryside with a castle in it.'

'The thing is …' Clyde looked uncomfortable; picked at his thumb.

'Stop that!' said Lizzi. 'You'll make it bleed.' Again, a smile lifted the corners of her mouth.

'The thing is … I'm sorry for what I said. I didn't mean it. I was upset and I was angry and I was worried –'

'You don't have to say sorry,' Lizzi interrupted.

'Yes, I do!' insisted Clyde. 'I was horrible and you only wanted to help me and you're the best person I've ever met and … I was horrible. So I'm sorry.'

'OK,' Lizzi murmured.

'OK,' said Clyde.

'Then I hope I don't make you cross again,' Lizzi added after a moment, 'when I tell you that I found your painting in the sketchpad.'

Clyde blinked at her; picked at his thumb again.

'I loved it, your Cloudgate,' she said. 'Everything about it. I loved it so much that I decided to drop it round to Mr Keller. I know I really shouldn't have without asking you, but that's what I did. And that's why I just called at your house. I wanted you to know that Mr Keller loved it, too.'

Something inside Clyde seemed to leap. He listened to Lizzi's words, but he couldn't answer. What she had said simply took his breath away.

Lizzi hesitated. She didn't want to pry. 'You've been

a bit lost, haven't you, Clyde?' she said gently. 'Trapped somewhere in the clouds? But what you've got to remember is that one day clouds always clear. And underneath is the beautiful blue sky.'

Clyde stood on the other side of the road from the church. He watched people arrive and disappear inside.

He saw Danny and Benny go in with Benny's mum and dad. Josie arrived with her parents, too, and a short while afterwards, John and Sarah.

He waited.

Suddenly he saw the boy he'd been looking for. He checked for traffic and ran across the road.

'Dave!'

Dave turned in the church doorway; did his best to hide his surprise.

'I was wondering ...' Clyde began. 'I've been thinking about what you said and I was wondering if ... well ... if I could come into church with you ... as it's Sunday and everything.'

Dave stared at him. 'Yeah!' he spluttered. 'Yeah, that'd be ... great!'

'Cool,' mumbled Clyde. 'Just one thing, though. Erm … do you think we could maybe sit at the back?'

A broad grin spread across Dave's face.

''Course we can. God's at the back, too, Clyde,' he said. 'God's everywhere.'

NATIONAL DISTRIBUTORS

UK: (and countries not listed below)

CWR, Waverley Abbey House, Waverley Lane, Farnham, Surrey GU9 8EP.

Tel: (01252) 784700 Outside UK (44) 1252 784700 Email: mail@cwr.org.uk

AUSTRALIA: KI Entertainment, Unit 21 317-321 Woodpark Road, Smithfield, New South Wales 2164.

Tel: 1 800 850 777 Fax: 02 9604 3699 Email: sales@kientertainment.com.au

CANADA: David C Cook Distribution Canada, PO Box 98, 55 Woodslee Avenue, Paris, Ontario N3L 3E5.

Tel: 1800 263 2664 Email: sandi.swanson@davidccook.ca

GHANA: Challenge Enterprises of Ghana, PO Box 5723, Accra.

Tel: (021) 222437/223249 Fax: (021) 226227 Email: ceg@africaonline.com.gh

HONG KONG: Cross Communications Ltd, 1/F, 562A Nathan Road, Kowloon.

Tel: 2780 1188 Fax: 2770 6229 Email: cross@crosshk.com

INDIA: Crystal Communications, 10-3-18/4/1, East Marredpalli, Secunderabad – 500026, Andhra Pradesh.

Tel/Fax: (040) 27737145 Email: crystal_edwj@rediffmail.com

KENYA: Keswick Books and Gifts Ltd, PO Box 10242-00400, Nairobi.

Tel: (020) 2226047/312639 Email: sales.keswick@africaonline.co.ke

MALAYSIA: Canaanland Distributors Sdn Bhd, No. 25 Jalan PJU 1A/41B, NZX Commercial Centre, Ara Jaya, 47301 Petaling Jaya, Selangor.

Tel: (03) 7885 0540/1/2 Fax: (03) 7885 0545 Email: info@canaanland.com.my

Salvation Publishing & Distribution Sdn Bhd, 23 Jalan SS 2/64, 47300 Petaling Jaya, Selangor.

Tel: (03) 78766411/78766797 Fax: (03) 78757066/78756360
Email: info@salvationbookcentre.com

NEW ZEALAND: KI Entertainment, Unit 21 317-321 Woodpark Road, Smithfield, New South Wales 2164, Australia.

Tel: 0 800 850 777 Fax: +612 9604 3699 Email: sales@kientertainment.com.au

NIGERIA: FBFM, Helen Baugh House, 96 St Finbarr's College Road, Akoka, Lagos.

Tel: (+234) 01-08075201777/08186337699/08154453905 Email: fbfm_1@yahoo.com

PHILIPPINES: OMF Literature Inc, 776 Boni Avenue, Mandaluyong City.

Tel: (02) 531 2183 Fax: (02) 531 1960 Email: gloadlaon@omflit.com

SINGAPORE: Alby Commercial Enterprises Pte Ltd, 95 Kallang Avenue #04-00, AIS Industrial Building, 339420.

Tel: (65) 629 27238 Fax: (65) 629 27235 Email: marketing@alby.com.sg

SRI LANKA: Christombu Publications (Pvt) Ltd, Bartleet House, 65 Braybrooke Place, Colombo 2.

Tel: (9411) 2421073/2447665 Email: christombupublications@gmail.com

USA: David C Cook Distribution Canada, PO Box 98, 55 Woodslee Avenue, Paris, Ontario N3L 3E5, Canada.

Tel: 1800 263 2664 Email: sandi.swanson@davidccook.ca

CWR is a Registered Charity – Number 294387

CWR is a Limited Company registered in England – Registration Number 1990308

More Topz SECRET STORIES!

Why not try the others in the series?

The *Topz Secret Stories* are full of fun and they also help you to discover things about yourself and God. The Dixons Gang present problems and opportunities to the Topz Gang.

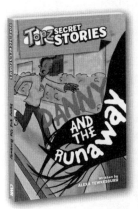

Danny and the Runaway
ISBN: 978-1-85345-991-7

There's lots of change in Holly Hill for members of the Topz and Dixons Gangs as Danny, Rick and Lily find that they have more in common than they first thought. Rick's dad left when he was only little, Danny's dad has moved overseas for a new job and now Lily has a stepdad – and it's a situation she's tempted to run away from. In this exciting Topz secret story, readers will be encouraged to remember that God really *can* work out all things in our lives for good – sometimes it just takes time to see the answers to our prayers.

One Too Many For Benny
ISBN: 978-1-85345-915-3
Pantomime Pandemonium
ISBN: 978-1-85345-916-0
Dixons' Den
ISBN: 978-1-85345-690-9
Dixons and the Wolf
ISBN: 978-1-85345-691-6

For current prices, visit **www.cwr.org.uk/store**
Available online or from Christian bookshops.

Topz Secret Diaries

These *Topz Secret Diaries* will help you discover things about yourself and God. Includes questions and quizzes, engaging puzzles, word searches, doodles, lists to write and more.

Boys Only
ISBN: 978-1-85345-596-4
126page paperback,
197x129mm

Just for Girls
ISBN: 978-1-85345-597-1
126page paperback,
197x129mm

Benny's Barmy Bits
ISBN: 978-1-85345-431-8

Danny's Daring Days
ISBN: 978-1-85345-502-5

Dave's Dizzy Doodles
ISBN: 978-1-85345-552-0

**Gruff & Saucy's
Topzy-Turvy Tales**
ISBN: 978-1-85345-553-7

John's Jam-Packed Jottings
ISBN: 978-1-85345-503-2

Josie's Jazzy Journal
ISBN: 978-1-85345-457-8

Paul's Potty Pages
ISBN: 978-1-85345-456-1

Sarah's Secret Scribblings
ISBN: 978-1-85345-432-5

Topz is a colourful daily devotional just for you

In each issue the Topz Gang teach you biblical truths through word games, puzzles, riddles, cartoons, competitions, simple prayers and daily Bible readings.

Available as an annual subscription
or as single issues.